MILTON'S COMUS

Copyright © 2007 BiblioBazaar
All rights reserved
ISBN: 978-1-4346-3246-3

Original copyright: 1891

John Milton

MILTON'S COMUS

With Introduction and Notes by
WILLIAM BELL, M.A.
PROFESSOR OF PHILOSOPHY AND LOGIC,
GOVERNMENT COLLEGE, LAHORE

MILTON'S COMUS

CONTENTS

INTRODUCTION. 9

COMUS. 19

NOTES... 55

INDEX TO THE NOTES 143

INTRODUCTION.

Few poems have been more variously designated than *Comus*. Milton himself describes it simply as "A Mask"; by others it has been criticised and estimated as a lyrical drama, a drama in the epic style, a lyric poem in the *form* of a play, a phantasy, an allegory, a philosophical poem, a suite of speeches or majestic soliloquies, and even a didactic poem. Such variety in the description of the poem is explained partly by its complex charm and many-sided interest, and partly by the desire to describe it from that point of view which should best reconcile its literary form with what we know of the genius and powers of its author. Those who, like Dr. Johnson, have blamed it as a drama, have admired it "as a series of lines," or as a lyric; one writer, who has found that its characters are nothing, its sentiments tedious, its story uninteresting, has nevertheless "doubted whether there will ever be any similar poem which gives so true a conception of the capacity and the dignity of the mind by which it was produced" (Bagehot's *Literary Studies*). Some who have praised it as an allegory see in it a satire on the evils both of the Church and of the State, while others regard it as alluding to the vices of the Court alone. Some have found its lyrical parts the best, while others, charmed with its "divine philosophy," have commended those deep conceits which place it alongside of the *Faerie Queen*, as shadowing forth an episode in the education of a noble soul and as a poet's lesson against intemperance and impurity. But no one can refuse to admit that, more than any other of Milton's shorter poems, it gives us an insight into the peculiar genius and character of its author: it was, in the opinion of Hallam, "sufficient to convince any one of taste and feeling that a great poet had arisen in England, and one partly formed in a different school from his contemporaries." It is true that in the early poems we do not find the whole of Milton, for he had yet to pass through many years of trouble and controversy;

but *Comus*, in a special degree, reveals or foreshadows much of the Milton of *Paradise Lost*. Whether we regard its place in Milton's life, in the series of his works, or in English literature as a whole, the poem is full of significance: it is worth while, therefore, to consider how its form was determined by the external circumstances and previous training of the poet; by his favourite studies in poetry, philosophy, history, and music; and by his noble theory of life in general, and of a poet's life in particular.

The mask was represented at Ludlow Castle on September 29th, 1634; it was probably composed early in that year. It belongs, therefore, to that group of poems *(L'Allegro, Il Penseroso, Arcades, Comus,* and *Lycidas*) written by Milton while living in his father's house at Horton, near Windsor, after having left the University of Cambridge in July, 1632. As he was born in 1608, he would be twenty-five years of age when this poem was composed. During his stay at Horton (1632-39), which was broken only by a journey to Italy in 1638-9, he was chiefly occupied with the study of the Greek, Roman, Italian, and English literatures, each of which has left its impress on *Comus*. He read widely and carefully, and it has been said that his great and original imagination was almost entirely nourished, or at least stimulated, by books: his residence at Horton was, accordingly, pre-eminently what he intended it to be, and what his father wisely and gladly permitted it to be—a time of preparation and ripening for the work to which he had dedicated himself. We are reminded of his own words in *Comus*:

> And Wisdom's self
> Oft seeks to sweet retired solitude,
> Where, with her best nurse, Contemplation,
> She plumes her feathers, and lets grow her wings,
> That, in the various bustle of resort,
> Were all to-ruffled, and sometimes impaired.

We find in *Comus* abundant reminiscences of Milton's study of the literature of antiquity. "It would not be too much to say that the literature of antiquity was to Milton's genius what soil and light are to a plant. It nourished, it coloured, it developed it. It determined not merely his character as an artist, but it exercised an influence on his intellect and temper scarcely less powerful than hereditary instincts and contemporary history. It at once animated and chastened his imagination; it modified his fancy; it furnished him with his models. On it his taste was formed; on it his style was moulded. From it his diction and his method derived their peculiarities. It transformed what would in all probability have been the mere counterpart of Caedmon's Paraphrase or Langland's Vision into Paradise Lost; and what would have been the mere counterpart of Corydon's Doleful Knell and the satire of the Three Estates, into Lycidas and Comus." *(Quarterly Review*, No. 326.)

But Milton has also told us that Spenser was his master, and the full charm of *Comus* cannot be realised without reference to the artistic and philosophical spirit of the author of the *Faerie Queene*. Both poems deal with the war between the body and the soul—between the lower and the higher nature. In an essay on 'Spenser as a philosophic poet,' De Vere says: "The perils and degradations of an animalised life are shown under the allegory of Sir Guyon's sea voyage with its successive storms and whirlpools, its 'rock of Reproach' strewn with wrecks and dead men's bones, its 'wandering islands,' its 'quicksands of Unthriftihead,' its 'whirlepoole of Decay,' its 'sea-monsters,' and lastly, its 'bower of Bliss,' and the doom which overtakes it, together with the deliverance of Acrasia's victims, transformed by that witch's spells into beasts. Still more powerful is the allegory of worldly ambition, illustrated under the name of 'the cave of Mammon.' The Legend of Holiness delineates with not less insight those enemies which wage war upon the spiritual life." All this Milton had studied in the *Faerie Queene*, and had understood it; and, like Sir Guyon, he felt himself to be a knight enrolled under the banner of Parity and Self-Control. So that, in *Comus*, we find the sovereign value of Temperance or Self-Regulation—what the Greeks called **σωφροσύνη**—set forth no less clearly than in Spenser's poem: in Milton's mask it becomes almost identical with Virtue itself. The enchantments of Acrasia in her Bower of Bliss become the spells of Comus; the armour of Belphoebe becomes the "complete steel" of Chastity; while the supremacy of Conscience, the bounty of Nature and man's ingratitude, the unloveliness of Mammon and of Excess, the blossom of Courtesy oft found on lowly stalk, and the final triumph of Virtue through striving and temptation, all are dwelt upon.

> It is the mind that maketh good or ill,
> That maketh wretch or happie, rich or poore:

so speaks Spenser; and Milton similarly—

> He that has light within his own clear breast
> May sit i' the centre, and enjoy bright day:
> But he that hides a dark soul and foul thoughts
> Benighted walks under the mid-day sun;
> Himself is his own dungeon.

In endeavouring still further to trace, by means of verbal or structural resemblances, the sources from which Milton drew his materials for *Comus*, critics have referred to Peele's *Old Wives' Tale* (1595); to Fletcher's pastoral, *The Faithful Shepherdess*, of which Charles Lamb has said that if all its parts 'had been in unison with its many innocent scenes and sweet lyric intermixtures, it had been a poem fit to vie with *Comus* or the *Arcadia*, to have been put into the hands of boys and virgins, to have made matter for young dreams, like the loves of Hermia and Lysander'; to Ben Jonson's mask of *Pleasure reconciled to Virtue* (1619), in which Comus is "the god of cheer, or the Belly"; and to the *Comus* of Erycius Puteanus (Henri du Puy), Professor of Eloquence at Louvain. It is true that Fletcher's pastoral was being acted in London about the time Milton was writing his *Comus*, that the poem by the Dutch Professor was republished at Oxford in 1634, and that resemblances are evident between Milton's poem and those named. But Professor Masson does well in warning us that "infinitely too much has been made of such coincidences. After all of them, even the most ideal and poetical, the feeling in reading *Comus* is that all here is different, all peculiar." Whatever Milton borrowed, he borrowed, as he says himself, in order to better it.

It is interesting to consider the mutual relations of the poems written by Milton at Horton. Everything that Milton wrote is Miltonic; he had what has been called the power of transforming everything into himself, and these poems are, accordingly, evidences of the development of Milton's opinions and of his secret purpose. It has been said that *L'Allegro* and *Il Penseroso* are to be regarded as "the pleadings, the decision on which is in Comus"—*L'Allegro* representing the Cavalier, and *Il Penseroso* the Puritan element. This is true only in a limited sense. It is true that the Puritan element in the Horton series of poems becomes more patent as we pass from the two lyrics to the mask of *Comus*, and from *Comus* to the elegy of *Lycidas*, just as, in the corresponding periods of time, the evils connected with the reign of Charles I. and with Laud's crusade against Puritanism were becoming more pronounced. But we can hardly regard Milton as having expressed any new decision in *Comus*: the decision is already made when "vain deluding Joys" are banished in *Il Penseroso*, and "loathed Melancholy" in *L'Allegro*. The mask is an expansion and exaltation of the delights of the contemplative man, but there is still a place for the "unreproved pleasures" of the cheerful man. Unless it were so, *Comus* could not have been written; there would have been no "sunshine holiday" for the rustics and no "victorious dance" for the gentle lady and her brothers. But in *Comus* we realise the mutual relation of *L'Allegro* and *Il Penseroso*; we see their application to the joys and sorrows of the actual life of individuals; we observe human nature in contact with the "hard assays" of life. And, subsequently, in *Lycidas* we are made to realise that this human nature is Milton's own, and to understand how it was that his Puritanism which, three years before, had permitted him to write a cavalier mask, should, three years after, lead him from the fresh fields of poetry into the barren plains of controversial prose.

The Mask was a favourite form of entertainment in England in Milton's youth, and had been so from the time of Henry VIII., in whose reign elaborate masked shows, introduced from Italy, first became popular. But they seem to have found their way into England, in a crude form, even earlier; and we read of court disguisings in the reign of Edward III. It is usually said that the Mask derives its name from the fact that the actors wore masks, and in Hall's Chronicle we read that, in 1512, "on the day of Epiphany at night, the king, with eleven others, was disguised after the manner of Italy, called a Mask, a thing not seen before in England; they were appareled in garments long and broad, wrought all with gold, with *visors* and caps of gold." The truth, however, seems to be that the use of a visor was not essential in such entertainments, which, from the first, were called 'masks,' the word 'masker' being used sometimes of the players, and sometimes of their disguises. The word has come to us, through the French form *masque*, cognate with Spanish *mascarada*, a masquerade or assembly of maskers, otherwise called a mummery. Up to the time of Henry VIII. these entertainments were of the nature of dumb-show or *tableaux vivants*, and delighted the spectators chiefly by the splendour of the costumes and machinery employed in their representation; but, afterwards, the chief actors spoke their parts, singing and dancing were introduced, and the composition of masks for royal and other courtly patrons became an occupation worthy of a poet. They were frequently combined with other forms of amusement, all of which were, in the case of the Court, placed under the management of a Master of Revels, whose official title was Magister Jocorum, Revellorum et *Mascorum*; in the first printed English tragedy, *Gorboduc* (1565), each act opens with what is called a dumb-show or mask. But the more elaborate form of the Mask soon grew to be an entertainment complete in itself, and the demand for such became so great in the time of James I. and Charles I. that the history of these reigns might almost be traced in the succession of masks then written. Ben Jonson, who thoroughly established the Mask in English literature, wrote many Court Masks, and made them a vehicle less for the display of 'painting and carpentry' than for the expression of the intellectual and social life of his time. His masks are excelled only by *Comus*, and possess in a high degree that 'Doric delicacy' in their songs and odes which Sir Henry Wotton found so ravishing in Milton's mask. Jonson, in his lifetime, declared that, next himself, only Fletcher and Chapman could write a mask; and apart from the compositions of these writers and of William Browne *(Inner Temple Masque)*, there are few specimens worthy to be named along with Jonson's until we come to Milton's *Arcades*. Other mask-writers were Middleton, Dekker, Shirley, Carew, and Davenant; and it is interesting to note that in Carew's *Coelum Brittanicum* (1633-4), for which Lawes composed the music, the two boys who afterwards acted in *Comus* had juvenile parts. It has been pointed out that the popularity of the Mask in Milton's youth received a stimulus from the Puritan hatred of the theatre which found expression at that time, and drove non-Puritans to welcome the Mask as a protest against that spirit which saw nothing but evil in every form of dramatic entertainment. Milton, who enjoyed the theatre—both "Jonson's learned sock" and what "ennobled hath the buskined stage"—was led, through his friendship with the musician Lawes, to compose a mask to celebrate the entry of the Earl of Bridgewater upon his office of "Lord President of the Council in the Principality of Wales and the Marches of the same." He had already written, also at the request of Lawes, a mask, or portion of a mask, called *Arcades*, and the success of this may have stimulated him to higher effort. The result was *Comus*, in which the Mask reached its highest level, and after which it practically faded out of our literature.

Milton's two masks, *Arcades* and *Comus*, were written for members of the same noble family, the former in honour of the Countess Dowager of Derby, and the latter in honour of John, first Earl of Bridgewater, who was both her stepson and son-in-law. This two-fold relation arose from the fact that the Earl was the son of Viscount Brackley, the Countess's second husband, and had himself married Lady Frances Stanley, a daughter of the Countess by her first husband, the fifth Earl of Derby. Amongst the children of the Earl of Bridgewater were three who took important parts in the representation of *Comus*—Alice, the youngest daughter, then about fourteen years of age, who appeared as *The Lady*; John, Viscount Brackley, who took the part of the *Elder Brother*, and Thomas Egerton, who appeared as the *Second Brother*. We do not know who acted the parts of *Comus* and *Sabrina*, but the part of the *Attendant Spirit* was taken by Henry Lawes, "gentleman of the Chapel Royal, and one of His Majesty's private musicians." The Earl's children were his pupils, and the mask was naturally produced under his direction. Milton's friendship with Lawes is shown by the sonnet which the poet addressed to the musician:

> Harry, whose tuneful and well measur'd song
> > First taught our English music how to span
> > Words with just note and accent, not to scan
> > With Midas' ears, committing short and long;
> Thy worth and skill exempts thee from the throng,
> > With praise enough for Envy to look wan;
> > To after age thou shalt be writ the man,
> That with smooth air could'st humour best our tongue.
> Thou honour'st Verse, and Verse must lend her wing
> > To honour thee, the priest of Phoebus' quire,
> > That tun'st their happiest lines in hymn, or story.

> Dante shall give Fame leave to set thee higher
> > Than his Casella, who he woo'd to sing,
> > Met in the milder shades of Purgatory.

We must remember also that it was to Lawes that Milton's *Comus* owed its first publication, and, as we see from the dedication prefixed to the text, that he was justly proud of his share in its first representation.

Such were the persons who appeared in Milton's mask; they are few in number, and the plan of the piece is correspondingly simple. There are three scenes which may be briefly characterised thus:

I. The Tempter and the Tempted: lines 1-658.
   Scene: A wild wood.
II. The Temptation and the Rescue: lines 659-958.
   Scene: The Palace of Comus.
III. The Triumph: lines 959-1023.
   Scene: The President's Castle.

In the first scene, after a kind of prologue (lines 1-92), the interest rises as we are introduced first to Comus and his rout, then to the Lady alone and "night-foundered," and finally to Comus and the Lady in company. At the same time the nature of the Lady's trial and her subsequent victory are foreshadowed in a conversation between the brothers and the attendant Spirit. This is one of the more Miltonic parts of the mask: in the philosophical reasoning of the elder brother, as opposed to the matter-of-fact arguments of the younger, we trace the young poet fresh from the study of the divine volume of Plato, and filled with a noble trust in God. In the second scene we breathe the unhallowed air of the abode of the wily tempter, who endeavours, "under fair pretence of friendly ends," to wind himself into the pure heart of the Lady. But his "gay rhetoric" is futile against the "sun-clad power of chastity"; and he is driven off the scene by the two brothers, who are led and instructed by the Spirit disguised as the shepherd Thyrsis. But the Lady, having been lured into the haunt of impurity, is left spell-bound, and appeal is made to the pure nymph Sabrina, who is "swift to aid a virgin, such as was herself, in hard-besetting need." It is in the contention between Comus and the Lady in this scene that the interest of the mask may be said to culminate, for here its purpose stands revealed: "it is a song to Temperance as the ground of Freedom, to temperance as the guard of all the virtues, to beauty as secured by temperance, and its central point and climax is in the pleading of these motives by the Lady against their opposites in the mouth of the Lord of sensual Revel." *Milton: Classical Writers*. In the third scene the Lady Alice and her brothers are presented by the Spirit to their noble father and mother as triumphing "in victorious dance o'er sensual folly and intemperance." The Spirit then speaks the epilogue, calling upon mortals who love true freedom to strive after virtue:

> Love Virtue; she alone is free.
> She can teach ye how to climb
> Higher than the sphery chime;
> Or, if Virtue feeble were,
> Heaven itself would stoop to her.

The last couplet Milton afterwards, on his Italian journey, entered in an album belonging to an Italian named Cerdogni, and underneath it the words, *Coelum non animum muto dum trans mare curro*, and his signature, Joannes Miltonius, Anglus. The juxtaposition of these verses is significant: though he had left his own land Milton had not become what, fifty or sixty years before, Roger Ascham had condemned as an "Italianated Englishman." He was one of those "worthy Gentlemen of England, whom all the Siren tongues of Italy could never untwine from the mast of God's word; nor no enchantment of vanity overturn them from the fear of God and love of honesty" (Ascham's *Scholemaster*). And one might almost infer that Milton, in his account of the sovereign plant Haemony which was to foil the wiles of *Comus*, had remembered not only Homer's description of the root Moly "that Hermes once to wise Ulysses gave,"[1] but also Ascham's remarks thereupon: "The true

---

[1] It is noteworthy that Lamb, whose allusiveness is remarkable, employs in his account of the plant Moly almost the exact words of Milton's description of Haemony; compare the following extract from *The Adventures of Ulysses* with lines 629-640 of *Comus*: "The flower of the herb Moly, which is sovereign against enchantments: the moly is a small unsightly root, its virtues but little known, and in low estimation; the dull shepherd treads on it every day with his clouted shoes, but it bears a small white flower, which is medicinal against charms, blights, mildews, and damps."

medicine against the enchantments of Circe, the vanity of licentious pleasure, the enticements of all sin, is, in Homer, the herb Moly, with the black root and white flower, sour at first, but sweet in the end; which Hesiod termeth the study of Virtue, hard and irksome in the beginning, but in the end easy and pleasant. And that which is most to be marvelled at, the divine poet Homer saith plainly that this medicine against sin and vanity is not found out by man, but given and taught by God." Milton's *Comus*, like his last great poems, is a poetical expression of the same belief. "His poetical works, the outcome of his inner life, his life of artistic contemplation, are," in the words of Prof. Dowden, "various renderings of one dominant idea—that the struggle for mastery between good and evil is the prime fact of life; and that a final victory of the righteous cause is assured by the existence of a divine order of the universe, which Milton knew by the name of 'Providence.'"

COMUS.

A MASK

PRESENTED AT LUDLOW CASTLE, 1634.

BEFORE

JOHN, EARL OF BRIDGEWATER,
THEN PRESIDENT OF WALES.

The Copy of a Letter written by Sir Henry Wotton to the Author upon the following Poem.

From the College, this 13 of April, 1638.

SIR,

It was a special favour, when you lately bestowed upon me here the first taste of your acquaintance, though no longer than to make me know that I wanted more time to value it, and to enjoy it rightly; and, in truth, if I could then have imagined your farther stay in these parts, which I understood afterwards by Mr. H., I would have been bold, in our vulgar phrase, to mend my draught (for you left me with an extreme thirst), and to have begged your conversation again, jointly with your said learned friend, at a poor meal or two, that we might have banded together some good authors of the antient time; among which I observed you to have been familiar.

Since your going, you have charged me with new obligations, both for a very kind letter from you dated the sixth of this month, and for a dainty piece of entertainment which came therewith.

Wherein I should much commend the tragical part, if the lyrical did not ravish me with a certain Doric delicacy in your songs and odes, whereunto I must plainly confess to have seen yet nothing parallel in our language: *Ipsa mollities*.[2] But I must not omit to tell you, that I now only owe you thanks for intimating unto me (how modestly soever) the true artificer. For the work itself I had viewed some good while before, with singular delight, having received it from our common friend Mr. R. in the very close of the late R.'s poems, printed at Oxford; whereunto it is added (as I now suppose) that the accessory might help out the principal, according to the art of stationers, and to leave the reader *con la bocca dolce*.[3]

Now, Sir, concerning your travels, wherein I may challenge a little more privilege of discourse with you; I suppose you will not blanch[4] Paris in your way; therefore I have been bold to trouble you with a few lines to Mr. M. B., whom you shall easily find attending the young Lord S. as his governor, and you may surely receive from him good directions for shaping of your farther journey into Italy, where he did reside by my choice some time for the king, after mine own recess from Venice.

I should think that your best line will be through the whole length of France to Marseilles, and thence by sea to Genoa, whence the passage into Tuscany is as diurnal as a Gravesend barge. I hasten, as you do, to Florence, or Siena, the rather to tell you a short story, from the interest you have given me in your safety.

At Siena I was tabled in the house of one Alberto Scipione, an old Roman courtier in dangerous times, having been steward to the Duca di Pagliano, who with all his family were strangled, save this only man, that escaped by foresight of the tempest. With him I had often much chat of those affairs; into which he took pleasure to look back from his native harbour; and at my departure toward Rome (which had been the centre of his experience) I had won confidence enough to beg his advice, how I might carry myself securely there, without offence of others, or of mine own conscience. *Signor Arrigo mio* (says he), *I pensieri stretti, ed il viso sciolto*,[5] will go safely over the whole world. Of which Delphian oracle (for

---
2   It is delicacy itself.
3   With a sweet taste in his mouth (so that he may desire more).
4   Avoid.
5   "Thoughts close, countenance open."

so I have found it) your judgment doth need no commentary; and therefore, Sir, I will commit you with it to the best of all securities, God's dear love, remaining

> Your friend as much to command
> as any of longer date,
>
> HENRY WOTTON.

Postscript.

Sir,—I have expressly sent this my footboy to prevent your departure without some acknowledgment from me of the receipt of your obliging letter, having myself through some business, I know not how, neglected the ordinary conveyance. In any part where I shall understand you fixed, I shall be glad and diligent to entertain you with home-novelties, even for some fomentation of our friendship, too soon interrupted in the cradle.[6]

TO THE RIGHT HONOURABLE[7]
JOHN, LORD VISCOUNT BRACKLEY,
Son and Heir-Apparent to the Earl of Bridgewater, etc.

MY LORD,

This Poem, which received its first occasion of birth from yourself and others of your noble family, and much honour from your own person in the performance, now returns again to make a final Dedication of itself to you. Although not openly acknowledged by the Author, yet it is a legitimate offspring, so lovely and so much desired that the often copying of it hath tired my pen to give my several friends satisfaction, and brought me to a necessity of producing it to the public view; and now to offer it up,

---

[6] This letter was printed in the edition of 1645, but omitted in that of 1673. It was written by Sir Henry Wotton, Provost of Eton College, just in time to overtake Milton before he set out on his journey to Italy. As a parting act of courtesy Milton had sent Sir Henry a letter with a copy of Lawes's edition of his *Comus*, and the above letter is an acknowledgment of the favour.

[7] Dedication of the anonymous edition of 1637: reprinted in the edition of 1645, but omitted in that of 1673.

in all rightful devotion, to those fair hopes and rare endowments of your much-promising youth, which give a full assurance to all that know you, of a future excellence. Live, sweet Lord, to be the honour of your name, and receive this as your own, from the hands of him who hath by many favours been long obliged to your most honoured Parents, and as in this representation your attendant *Thyrsis*,[8] so now in all real expression,

Your faithful and most humble Servant,
H. LAWES.

---

8   See Notes, line 494.

THE PERSONS.

The ATTENDANT SPIRIT, Afterwards In The Habit Of THYRSIS.
COMUS, With His Crew.
The LADY.
FIRST BROTHER.
SECOND BROTHER.
SABRINA, The Nymph.

The Chief Persons Which Presented Were:—
    The Lord Brackley;
    Mr. Thomas Egerton, His Brother;
    The Lady Alice Egerton.

COMUS.

The first Scene discovers a wild wood.

The ATTENDANT SPIRIT *descends or enters.*
    Before the starry threshold of Jove's court
My mansion is, where those immortal shapes
Of bright aërial spirits live insphered
In regions mild of calm and serene air,
Above the smoke and stir of this dim spot
Which men call Earth, and, with low-thoughted care,
Confined and pestered in this pinfold here,
Strive to keep up a frail and feverish being,
Unmindful of the crown that Virtue gives,
After this mortal change, to her true servants   10
Amongst the enthroned gods on sainted seats.
Yet some there be that by due steps aspire
To lay their just hands on that golden key
That opes the palace of eternity.
To such my errand is; and, but for such,
I would not soil these pure ambrosial weeds
With the rank vapours of this sin-worn mould.
    But to my task. Neptune, besides the sway
Of every salt flood and each ebbing stream,
Took in by lot, 'twixt high and nether Jove,   20
Imperial rule of all the sea-girt isles
That, like to rich and various gems, inlay
The unadornéd bosom of the deep;
Which he, to grace his tributary gods,
By course commits to several government,
And gives them leave to wear their sapphire crowns

And wield their little tridents. But this Isle,
The greatest and the best of all the main,
He quarters to his blue-haired deities;
And all this tract that fronts the falling sun   30
A noble Peer of mickle trust and power
Has in his charge, with tempered awe to guide
An old and haughty nation, proud in arms:
Where his fair offspring, nursed in princely lore,
Are coming to attend their father's state,
And new-intrusted sceptre. But their way
Lies through the perplexed paths of this drear wood,
The nodding horror of whose shady brows
Threats the forlorn and wandering passenger;
And here their tender age might suffer peril,   40
But that, by quick command from sovran Jove,
I was despatched for their defence and guard:
And listen why; for I will tell you now
What never yet was heard in tale or song,
From old or modern bard, in hall or bower.

    Bacchus, that first from out the purple grape
Crushed the sweet poison of misuséd wine,
After the Tuscan mariners transformed,
Coasting the Tyrrhene shore, as the winds listed,
On Circe's island fell: (who knows not Circe,   0
The daughter of the Sun, whose charmèd cup
Whoever tasted lost his upright shape,
And downward fell into a grovelling swine?)
This Nymph, that gazed upon his clustering locks,
With ivy berries wreathed, and his blithe youth,
Had by him, ere he parted thence, a son
Much like his father, but his mother more,
Whom therefore she brought up, and Comus named:
Who, ripe and frolic of his full-grown age,
Roving the Celtic and Iberian fields,   60
At last betakes him to this ominous wood,
And, in thick shelter of black shades imbowered,
Excels his mother at her mighty art;
Offering to every weary traveller
His orient liquor in a crystal glass,

To quench the drouth of Phoebus; which as they taste
(For most do taste through fond intemperate thirst),
Soon as the potion works, their human count'nance,
The express resemblance of the gods, is changed
Into some brutish form of wolf or bear,   70
Or ounce or tiger, hog, or bearded goat,
All other parts remaining as they were.
And they, so perfect is their misery,
Not once perceive their foul disfigurement,
But boast themselves more comely than before,
And all their friends and native home forget,
To roll with pleasure in a sensual sty.
Therefore, when any favoured of high Jove
Chances to pass through this adventurous glade,
Swift as the sparkle of a glancing star   80
I shoot from heaven, to give him safe convoy,
As now I do. But first I must put off
These my sky-robes, spun out of Iris' woof,
And take the weeds and likeness of a swain
That to the service of this house belongs,
Who, with his soft pipe and smooth-dittied song,
Well knows to still the wild winds when they roar,
And hush the waving woods; nor of less faith,
And in this office of his mountain watch
Likeliest, and nearest to the present aid   90
Of this occasion. But I hear the tread
Of hateful steps; I must be viewless now.

COMUS *enters, with a charming-rod in one hand, his glass in the other; with him a rout of monsters, headed like sundry sorts of wild beasts, but otherwise like men and women, their apparel glistering. They come in making a riotous and unruly noise, with torches in their hands.*

Comus. The star that bids the shepherd fold
Now the top of heaven doth hold;
And the gilded car of day
His glowing axle doth allay
In the steep Atlantic stream;
And the slope sun his upward beam

Shoots against the dusky pole,
Pacing toward the other goal 100
Of his chamber in the east.
Meanwhile, welcome joy and feast,
Midnight shout and revelry,
Tipsy dance and jollity.
Braid your locks with rosy twine,
Dropping odours, dropping wine.
Rigour now is gone to bed;
And Advice with scrupulous head,
Strict Age, and sour Severity,
With their grave saws, in slumber lie. 110
We, that are of purer fire,
Imitate the starry quire,
Who, in their nightly watchful spheres,
Lead in swift round the months and years.
The sounds and seas, with all their finny drove,
Now to the moon in wavering morrice move;
And on the tawny sands and shelves
Trip the pert fairies and the dapper elves.
By dimpled brook and fountain-brim,
The wood-nymphs, decked with daisies trim, 120
Their merry wakes and pastimes keep:
What hath night to do with sleep?
Night hath better sweets to prove;
Venus now wakes, and wakens Love.
Come, let us our rights begin;
'Tis only daylight that makes sin,
Which these dun shades will ne'er report.
Hail, goddess of nocturnal sport,
Dark-veiled Cotytto, to whom the secret flame
Of midnight torches burns! mysterious dame, 130
That ne'er art called but when the dragon womb
Of Stygian darkness spets her thickest gloom,
And makes one blot of all the air!
Stay thy cloudy ebon chair,
Wherein thou ridest with Hecat', and befriend
Us thy vowed priests, till utmost end
Of all thy dues be done, and none left out,

    Ere the blabbing eastern scout,
    The nice Morn on the Indian steep,
    From her cabined loop-hole peep,   140
    And to the tell-tale Sun descry
    Our concealed solemnity.
    Come, knit hands, and beat the ground
    In a light fantastic round.   *[The Measure.*
      Break off, break off! I feel the different pace
    Of some chaste footing near about this ground.
    Run to your shrouds within these brakes and trees;
    Our number may affright. Some virgin sure
    (For so I can distinguish by mine art)
    Benighted in these woods! Now to my charms,   150
    And to my wily trains: I shall ere long
    Be well stocked with as fair a herd as grazed
    About my mother Circe. Thus I hurl
    My dazzling spells into the spongy air,
    Of power to cheat the eye with blear illusion,
    And give it false presentments, lest the place
    And my quaint habits breed astonishment,
    And put the damsel to suspicious flight;
    Which must not be, for that's against my course.
    I, under fair pretence of friendly ends,   160
    And well-placed words of glozing courtesy,
    Baited with reasons not unplausible,
    Wind me into the easy-hearted man,
    And hug him into snares. When once her eye
    Hath met the virtue of this magic dust,
    I shall appear some harmless villager
    Whom thrift keeps up about his country gear.
    But here she comes; I fairly step aside,
    And hearken, if I may, her business here.

The LADY enters.
    Lady. This way the noise was, if mine ear be true,
    My best guide now. Methought it was the sound
    Of riot and ill-managed merriment,   172
    Such as the jocund flute or gamesome pipe
    Stirs up among the loose unlettered hinds,

When, for their teeming flocks and granges full,
In wanton dance they praise the bounteous Pan,
And thank the gods amiss. I should be loth
To meet the rudeness and swilled insolence
Of such late wassailers; yet, oh! where else
Shall I inform my unacquainted feet   180
In the blind mazes of this tangled wood?
My brothers, when they saw me wearied out
With this long way, resolving here to lodge
Under the spreading favour of these pines,
Stepped, as they said, to the next thicket-side
To bring me berries, or such cooling fruit
As the kind hospitable woods provide.
They left me then when the grey-hooded Even,
Like a sad votarist in palmer's weed,
Rose from the hindmost wheels of Phoebus' wain.   190
But where they are, and why they came not back,
Is now the labour of my thoughts. 'Tis likeliest
They had engaged their wandering steps too far;
And envious darkness, ere they could return,
Had stole them from me. Else, O thievish Night,
Why shouldst thou, but for some felonious end,
In thy dark lantern thus close up the stars
That Nature hung in heaven, and filled their lamps
With everlasting oil to give due light
To the misled and lonely traveller?   200
This is the place, as well as I may guess,
Whence even now the tumult of loud mirth
Was rife, and perfect in my listening ear;
Yet nought but single darkness do I find.
What might this be? A thousand fantasies
Begin to throng into my memory,
Of calling shapes, and beckoning shadows dire,
And airy tongues that syllable men's names
On sands and shores and desert wildernesses.
These thoughts may startle well, but not astound   210
The virtuous mind, that ever walks attended
By a strong siding champion, Conscience.
O, welcome, pure-eyed Faith, white-handed Hope,

Thou hovering angel girt with golden wings,
And thou unblemished form of Chastity!
I see ye visibly, and now believe
That He, the Supreme Good, to whom all things ill
Are but as slavish officers of vengeance,
Would send a glistering guardian, if need were,
To keep my life and honour unassailed . . . 220
Was I deceived, or did a sable cloud
Turn forth her silver lining on the night?
I did not err: there does a sable cloud
Turn forth her silver lining on the night,
And casts a gleam over this tufted grove.
I cannot hallo to my brothers, but
Such noise as I can make to be heard farthest
I'll venture; for my new-enlivened spirits
Prompt me, and they perhaps are not far off.

Song.
   Sweet Echo, sweetest nymph, that liv'st unseen 230
      Within thy airy shell
    By slow Meander's margent green,
  And in the violet-embroidered vale
    Where the love-lorn nightingale
  Nightly to thee her sad song mourneth well:
  Canst thou not tell me of a gentle pair
    That likest thy Narcissus are?
      O, if thou have
    Hid them in some flowery cave,
     Tell me but where, 240
   Sweet Queen of Parley, Daughter of the Sphere!
  So may'st thou be translated to the skies,
And give resounding grace to all Heaven's harmonies!

Comus. Can any mortal mixture of earth's mould
  Breathe such divine enchanting ravishment?
  Sure something holy lodges in that breast,
  And with these raptures moves the vocal air
  To testify his hidden residence.

How sweetly did they float upon the wings
Of silence, through the empty-vaulted night, 250
At every fall smoothing the raven down
Of darkness till it smiled! I have oft heard
My mother Circe with the Sirens three,
Amidst the flowery-kirtled Naiades,
Culling their potent herbs and baleful drugs,
Who, as they sung, would take the prisoned soul,
And lap it in Elysium: Scylla wept,
And chid her barking waves into attention,
And fell Charybdis murmured soft applause.
Yet they in pleasing slumber lulled the sense, 260
And in sweet madness robbed it of itself;
But such a sacred and home-felt delight,
Such sober certainty of waking bliss,
I never heard till now. I'll speak to her,
And she shall be my queen.—Hail, foreign wonder!
Whom certain these rough shades did never breed,
Unless the goddess that in rural shrine
Dwell'st here with Pan or Sylvan by blest song
Forbidding every bleak unkindly fog
To touch the prosperous growth of this tall wood. 270

Lady. Nay, gentle shepherd, ill is lost that praise
    That is addressed to unattending ears.
    Not any boast of skill, but extreme shift
    How to regain my severed company,
    Compelled me to awake the courteous Echo
    To give me answer from her mossy couch.

Comus. What chance, good Lady, hath bereft you thus?

Lady. Dim darkness and this leafy labyrinth.

Comus. Could that divide you from near-ushering guides?

Lady. They left me weary on a grassy turf. 280

Comus. By falsehood, or discourtesy, or why?

Lady. To seek i' the valley some cool friendly spring.

Comus. And left your fair side all unguarded, lady?

Lady. They were but twain, and purposed quick return.

Comus. Perhaps forestalling night prevented them.

Lady. How easy my misfortune is to hit!

Comus. Imports their loss, beside the present need?

Lady. No less than if I should my brothers lose.

Comus. Were they of manly prime, or youthful bloom?

Lady. As smooth as Hebe's their unrazored lips. 290

Comus. Two such I saw, what time the laboured ox
    In his loose traces from the furrow came,
    And the swinked hedger at his supper sat.
    I saw them under a green mantling vine,
    That crawls along the side of yon small hill,
    Plucking ripe clusters from the tender shoots;
    Their port was more than human, as they stood
    I took it for a faery vision
    Of some gay creatures of the element,
    That in the colours of the rainbow live, 300
    And play i' the plighted clouds. I was awe-strook,
    And, as I passed, I worshiped. If those you seek,
    It were a journey like the path to Heaven
    To help you find them.

Lady.   Gentle villager,
    What readiest way would bring me to that place?
Comus. Due west it rises from this shrubby point.
Lady. To find out that, good shepherd, I suppose,
    In such a scant allowance of star-light,
    Would overtask the best land-pilot's art,
    Without the sure guess of well-practised feet. 310

Comus. I know each lane, and every alley green,
    Dingle, or bushy dell, of this wild wood,
    And every bosky bourn from side to side,
    My daily walks and ancient neighbourhood;

And, if your stray attendance be yet lodged,
Or shroud within these limits, I shall know
Ere morrow wake, or the low-roosted lark
From her thatched pallet rouse. If otherwise,
I can conduct you, lady, to a low
But loyal cottage, where you may be safe   320
Till further quest.

Lady.   Shepherd, I take thy word,
And trust thy honest-offered courtesy,
Which oft is sooner found in lowly sheds,
With smoky rafters, than in tapestry halls
And courts of princes, where it first was named,
And yet is most pretended. In a place
Less warranted than this, or less secure,
I cannot be, that I should fear to change it.
Eye me, blest Providence, and square my trial
To my proportioned strength! Shepherd, lead on.

[Exeunt.

Enter the Two Brothers.

Elder Brother. Unmuffle, ye faint stars; and thou, fair moon,   331
That wont'st to love the traveller's benison,
Stoop thy pale visage through an amber cloud,
And disinherit Chaos, that reigns here
In double night of darkness and of shades;
Or, if your influence be quite dammed up
With black usurping mists, some gentle taper,
Though a rush-candle from the wicker hole
Of some clay habitation, visit us
With thy long levelled rule of streaming light,   340
And thou shalt be our star of Arcady,
Or Tyrian Cynosure.

Second Brother.   Or, if our eyes
Be barred that happiness, might we but hear
The folded flocks, penned in their wattled cotes,

Or sound of pastoral reed with oaten stops,
Or whistle from the lodge, or village cock
Count the night-watches to his feathery dames,
'Twould be some solace yet, some little cheering,
In this close dungeon of innumerous boughs.
But, Oh, that hapless virgin, our lost sister! 350
Where may she wander now, whither betake her
From the chill dew, amongst rude burs and thistles?
Perhaps some cold bank is her bolster now,
Or 'gainst the rugged bark of some broad elm
Leans her unpillowed head, fraught with sad fears.
What if in wild amazement and affright,
Or, while we speak, within the direful grasp
Of savage hunger, or of savage heat!

Elder Brother. Peace, brother: be not over-exquisite
To cast the fashion of uncertain evils; 360
For, grant they be so, while they rest unknown,
What need a man forestall his date of grief,
And run to meet what he would most avoid?
Or, if they be but false alarms of fear,
How bitter is such self-delusion!
I do not think my sister so to seek,
Or so unprincipled in virtue's book,
And the sweet peace that goodness bosoms ever,
As that the single want of light and noise
(Not being in danger, as I trust she is not) 370
Could stir the constant mood of her calm thoughts,
And put them into misbecoming plight.
Virtue could see to do what Virtue would
By her own radiant light, though sun and moon
Were in the flat sea sunk. And Wisdom's self
Oft seeks to sweet retired solitude,
Where, with her best nurse, Contemplation,
She plumes her feathers, and lets grow her wings,
That, in the various bustle of resort,
Were all to-ruffled, and sometimes impaired. 380
He that has light within his own clear breast
May sit i' the centre, and enjoy bright day:

But he that hides a dark soul and foul thoughts
Benighted walks under the mid-day sun;
Himself is his own dungeon.

Second Brother.   'Tis most true
That musing meditation most affects
The pensive secrecy of desert cell,
Far from the cheerful haunt of men and herds,
And sits as safe as in a senate-house;
For who would rob a hermit of his weeds,   390
His few books, or his beads, or maple dish,
Or do his grey hairs any violence?
But Beauty, like the fair Hesperian tree
Laden with blooming gold, had need the guard
Of dragon-watch with unenchanted eye
To save her blossoms, and defend her fruit,
From the rash hand of bold Incontinence.
You may as well spread out the unsunned heaps
Of miser's treasure by an outlaw's den,
And tell me it is safe, as bid me hope   400
Danger will wink on Opportunity,
And let a single helpless maiden pass
Uninjured in this wild surrounding waste.
Of night or loneliness it recks me not;
I fear the dread events that dog them both,
Lest some ill-greeting touch attempt the person
Of our unownéd sister.

Elder Brother.   I do not, brother,
Infer as if I thought my sister's state
Secure without all doubt or controversy;
Yet, where an equal poise of hope and fear   410
Does arbitrate the event, my nature is
That I incline to hope rather than fear,
And gladly banish squint suspicion.
My sister is not so defenceless left
As you imagine; she has a hidden strength,
Which you remember not.

Second Brother.   What hidden strength,
    Unless the strength of Heaven, if you mean that?

Elder Brother. I mean that too, but yet a hidden strength,
    Which, if Heaven gave it, may be termed her own.
    'Tis chastity, my brother, chastity: 420
    She that has that is clad in cómplete steel,
    And, like a quivered nymph with arrows keen,
    May trace huge forests, and unharboured heaths,
    Infámous hills, and sandy perilous wilds;
    Where, through the sacred rays of chastity,
    No savage fierce, bandite, or mountaineer,
    Will dare to soil her virgin purity.
    Yea, there where very desolation dwells,
    By grots and caverns shagged with horrid shades,
    She may pass on with unblenched majesty,   430
    Be it not done in pride, or in presumption.
    Some say no evil thing that walks by night,
    In fog or fire, by lake or moorish fen,
    Blue meagre hag, or stubborn unlaid ghost,
    That breaks his magic chains at curfew time,
    No goblin or swart faery of the mine,
    Hath hurtful power o'er true virginity.
    Do ye believe me yet, or shall I call
    Antiquity from the old schools of Greece
    To testify the arms of chastity?   440
    Hence had the huntress Dian her dread bow
    Fair silver-shafted queen for ever chaste,
    Wherewith she tamed the brinded lioness
    And spotted mountain-pard, but set at nought
    The frivolous bolt of Cupid; gods and men
    Feared her stern frown, and she was queen o' the woods.
    What was that snaky-headed Gorgon shield
    That wise Minerva wore, unconquered virgin,
    Wherewith she freezed her foes to congealed stone,
    But rigid looks of chaste austerity,   450
    And noble grace that dashed brute violence
    With sudden adoration and blank awe?
    So dear to Heaven is saintly chastity

That, when a soul is found sincerely so,
A thousand liveried angels lackey her,
Driving far off each thing of sin and guilt,
And in clear dream and solemn vision
Tell her of things that no gross ear can hear;
Till oft converse with heavenly habitants
Begin to cast a beam on the outward shape, 460
The unpolluted temple of the mind,
And turns it by degrees to the soul's essence,
Till all be made immortal. But, when lust,
By unchaste looks, loose gestures, and foul talk,
But most by lewd and lavish act of sin,
Lets in defilement to the inward parts,
The soul grows clotted by contagion,
Imbodies, and imbrutes, till she quite loose
The divine property of her first being.
Such are those thick and gloomy shadows damp 470
Oft seen in charnel-vaults and sepulchres,
Lingering and sitting by a new-made grave,
As loth to leave the body that it loved,
And linked itself by carnal sensualty
To a degenerate and degraded state.
Second Brother. How charming is divine Philosophy!
Not harsh and crabbed, as dull fools suppose,
But musical as is Apollo's lute,
And a perpetual feast of nectared sweets,
Where no crude surfeit reigns.

Elder Brother.   List! list! I hear 480
  Some far-off hallo break the silent air.

Second Brother. Methought so too; what should it be?

Elder Brother.   For certain,
  Either some one, like us, night-foundered here,
  Or else some neighbour woodman, or, at worst,
  Some roving robber calling to his fellows.
  Second Brother. Heaven keep my sister! Again, again, and near!
  Best draw, and stand upon our guard.

Elder Brother. I'll hallo.
>If he be friendly, he comes well: if not,
>Defence is a good cause, and Heaven be for us!

Enter the ATTENDANT SPIRIT, *habited like a shepherd.*

>That hallo I should know. What are you? speak. 490
>Come not too near; you fall on iron stakes else.

Spirit. What voice is that? my young Lord? speak again.

Second Brother. O brother, 'tis my father's shepherd, sure.

Elder Brother. Thyrsis! whose artful strains have oft delayed
>The huddling brook to hear his madrigal,
>And sweetened every musk rose of the dale.
>How camest thou here, good swain? Hath any ram
>Slipped from the fold, or young kid lost his dam,
>Or straggling wether the pent flock forsook?
>How couldst thou find this dark sequestered nook? 500

Spirit. O my loved master's heir, and his next joy,
>I came not here on such a trivial toy
>As a strayed ewe, or to pursue the stealth
>Of pilfering wolf; not all the fleecy wealth
>That doth enrich these downs is worth a thought
>To this my errand, and the care it brought,
>But, oh! my virgin Lady, where is she?
>How chance she is not in your company?

Elder Brother. To tell thee sadly, Shepherd, without blame
>Or our neglect, we lost her as we came. 510

Spirit. Ay me unhappy! then my fears are true.

Elder Brother. What fears, good Thyrsis? Prithee briefly shew.

Spirit. I'll tell ye. 'Tis not vain or fabulous
>(Though so esteemed by shallow ignorance)
>What the sage poets, taught by the heavenly Muse,
>Storied of old in high immortal verse
>Of dire Chimeras and enchanted isles,

And rifted rocks whose entrance leads to Hell;
For such there be, but unbelief is blind.
    Within the navel of this hideous wood,   520
Immured in cypress shades, a sorcerer dwells,
Of Bacchus and of Circe born, great Comus,
Deep skilled in all his mother's witcheries,
And here to every thirsty wanderer
By sly enticement gives his baneful cup,
With many murmurs mixed, whose pleasing poison
The visage quite transforms of him that drinks,
And the inglorious likeness of a beast
Fixes instead, unmoulding reason's mintage
Charáctered in the face. This have I learnt   530
Tending my flocks hard by i' the hilly crofts
That brow this bottom glade; whence night by night
He and his monstrous rout are heard to howl
Like stabled wolves, or tigers at their prey,
Doing abhorred rites to Hecate
In their obscuréd haunts of inmost bowers.
Yet have they many baits and guileful spells
To inveigle and invite the unwary sense
Of them that pass unweeting by the way.
This evening late, by then the chewing flocks   540
Had ta'en their supper on the savoury herb
Of knot-grass dew-besprent, and were in fold,
I sat me down to watch upon a bank
With ivy canopied, and interwove
With flaunting honeysuckle, and began,
Wrapt in a pleasing fit of melancholy,
To meditate my rural minstrelsy,
Till fancy had her fill. But ere a close
The wonted roar was up amidst the woods,
And filled the air with barbarous dissonance;   550
At which I ceased, and listened them awhile,
Till an unusual stop of sudden silence
Gave respite to the drowsy frighted steeds
That draw the litter of close-curtained Sleep.
At last a soft and solemn-breathing sound
Rose like a steam of rich distilled perfumes,

And stole upon the air, that even Silence
Was took ere she was ware, and wished she might
Deny her nature, and be never more,
Still to be so displaced. I was all ear, 560
And took in strains that might create a soul
Under the ribs of Death. But, oh! ere long
Too well I did perceive it was the voice
Of my most honoured Lady, your dear sister.
Amazed I stood, harrowed with grief and fear;
And "O poor hapless nightingale," thought I,
"How sweet thou sing'st, how near the deadly snare!"
Then down the lawns I ran with headlong haste,
Through paths and turnings often trod by day,
Till, guided by mine ear, I found the place 570
Where that damned wizard, hid in sly disguise
(For so by certain signs I knew), had met
Already, ere my best speed could prevent,
The aidless innocent lady, his wished prey;
Who gently asked if he had seen such two,
Supposing him some neighbour villager.
Longer I durst not stay, but soon I guessed
Ye were the two she meant; with that I sprung
Into swift flight, till I had found you here;
But further know I not.

Second Brother. O night and shades, 580
How are ye joined with hell in triple knot
Against the unarmed weakness of one virgin,
Alone and helpless! Is this the confidence
You gave me, brother?

Elder Brother. Yes, and keep it still;
Lean on it safely; not a period
Shall be unsaid for me. Against the threats
Of malice or of sorcery, or that power
Which erring men call Chance, this I hold firm:
Virtue may be assailed, but never hurt,
Surprised by unjust force, but not enthralled; 590
Yea, even that which Mischief meant most harm

    Shall in the happy trial prove most glory.
    But evil on itself shall back recoil,
    And mix no more with goodness, when at last,
    Gathered like scum, and settled to itself,
    It shall be in eternal restless change
    Self-fed and self-consumed. If this fail,
    The pillared firmament is rottenness,
    And earth's base built on stubble. But come, let's on!
    Against the opposing will and arm of Heaven   600
    May never this just sword be lifted up;
    But, for that damned magician, let him be girt
    With all the grisly legions that troop
    Under the sooty flag of Acheron,
    Harpies and Hydras, or all the monstrous forms
    'Twixt Africa and Ind, I'll find him out,
    And force him to return his purchase back,
    Or drag him by the curls to a foul death,
    Cursed as his life.

Spirit.   Alas! good venturous youth,
    I love thy courage yet, and bold emprise;   610
    But here thy sword can do thee little stead.
    Far other arms and other weapons must
    Be those that quell the might of hellish charms.
    He with his bare wand can unthread thy joints,
    And crumble all thy sinews.

Elder Brother.   Why, prithee, Shepherd,
    How durst thou then thyself approach so near
    As to make this relation?

Spirit.   Care and utmost shifts
    How to secure the Lady from surprisal
    Brought to my mind a certain shepherd lad,
    Of small regard to see to, yet well skilled   620
    In every virtuous plant and healing herb
    That spreads her verdant leaf to the morning ray.
    He loved me well, and oft would beg me sing;
    Which when I did, he on the tender grass
    Would sit, and hearken even to ecstasy,

And in requital ope his leathern scrip,
And show me simples of a thousand names,
Telling their strange and vigorous faculties.
Amongst the rest a small unsightly root,
But of divine effect, he culled me out. 630
The leaf was darkish, and had prickles on it,
But in another country, as he said,
Bore a bright golden flower, but not in this soil:
Unknown, and like esteemed, and the dull swain
Treads on it daily with his clouted shoon;
And yet more med'cinal is it than that Moly
That Hermes once to wise Ulysses gave.
He called it Hæmony, and gave it me,
And bade me keep it as of sovran use
'Gainst all enchantments, mildew blast, or damp, 640
Or ghastly Furies' apparition.
I pursed it up, but little reckoning made,
Till now that this extremity compelled.
But now I find it true; for by this means
I knew the foul enchanter, though disguised,
Entered the very lime-twigs of his spells,
And yet came off. If you have this about you
(As I will give you when we go) you may
Boldly assault the necromancer's hall;
Where if he be, with dauntless hardihood 650
And brandished blade rush on him: break his glass,
And shed the luscious liquor on the ground;
But seize his wand. Though he and his curst crew
Fierce sign of battle make, and menace high,
Or, like the sons of Vulcan, vomit smoke,
Yet will they soon retire, if he but shrink.

Elder Brother. Thyrsis, lead on apace; I'll follow thee;
And some good angel bear a shield before us!

The Scene changes to a stately palace, set out with all manner of deliciousness: soft music, tables spread with all dainties. COMUS *appears with his rabble, and the* LADY *set in an enchanted chair: to whom he offers his glass; which she puts by, and goes about to rise.*

Comus. Nay, lady, sit. If I but wave this wand,
    Your nerves are all chained up in alabaster,   660
    And you a statue, or as Daphne was,
    Root-bound, that fled Apollo.

Lady.   Fool, do not boast.
    Thou canst not touch the freedom of my mind
    With all thy charms, although this corporal rind
    Thou hast immanacled while Heaven sees good.
Comus. Why are you vexed, lady? why do you frown?
    Here dwell no frowns, nor anger; from these gates
    Sorrow flies far. See, here be all the pleasures
    That fancy can beget on youthful thoughts,
    When the fresh blood grows lively, and returns   670
    Brisk as the April buds in primrose season.
    And first behold this cordial julep here,
    That flames and dances in his crystal bounds,
    With spirits of balm and fragrant syrups mixed.
    Not that Nepenthes which the wife of Thone
    In Egypt gave to Jove-born Helena
    Is of such power to stir up joy as this,
    To life so friendly, or so cool to thirst.
    Why should you be so cruel to yourself,
    And to those dainty limbs, which Nature lent   680
    For gentle usage and soft delicacy?
    But you invert the covenants of her trust,
    And harshly deal, like an ill borrower,
    With that which you received on other terms,
    Scorning the unexempt condition
    By which all mortal frailty must subsist,
    Refreshment after toil, ease after pain,
    That have been tired all day without repast,
    And timely rest have wanted. But, fair virgin,
    This will restore all soon.

Lady.   'Twill not, false traitor!   690
    'Twill not restore the truth and honesty
    That thou hast banished from thy tongue with lies.
    Was this the cottage and the safe abode

    Thou told'st me of? What grim aspects are these,
    These oughly-headed monsters? Mercy guard me!
    Hence with thy brewed enchantments, foul deceiver!
    Hast thou betrayed my credulous innocence
    With vizored falsehood and base forgery?
    And would'st thou seek again to trap me here
    With liquorish baits, fit to ensnare a brute?   700
    Were it a draught for Juno when she banquets,
    I would not taste thy treasonous offer. None
    But such as are good men can give good things;
    And that which is not good is not delicious
    To a well-governed and wise appetite.

Comus. O foolishness of men! that lend their ears
    To those budge doctors of the Stoic fur,
    And fetch their precepts from the Cynic tub,
    Praising the lean and sallow Abstinence!
    Wherefore did Nature pour her bounties forth   710
    With such a full and unwithdrawing hand,
    Covering the earth with odours, fruits, and flocks,
    Thronging the seas with spawn innumerable,
    But all to please and sate the curious taste?
    And set to work millions of spinning worms,
    That in their green shops weave the smooth-haired silk,
    To deck her sons; and, that no corner might
    Be vacant of her plenty, in her own loins
    She hutched the all-worshipped ore and precious gems,
    To store her children with. If all the world   720
    Should, in a pet of temperance, feed on pulse,
    Drink the clear stream, and nothing wear but frieze,
    The All-giver would be unthanked, would be unpraised,
    Not half his riches known, and yet despised;
    And we should serve him as a grudging master,
    As a penurious niggard of his wealth,
    And live like Nature's bastards, not her sons,
    Who would be quite surcharged with her own weight,
    And strangled with her waste fertility:
    The earth cumbered, and the winged air darked with plumes, 730
    The herds would over-multitude their lords;

    The sea o'erfraught would swell, and the unsought diamonds
    Would so emblaze the forehead of the deep,
    And so bestud with stars, that they below
    Would grow inured to light, and come at last
    To gaze upon the sun with shameless brows.
    List, lady; be not coy, and be not cozened
    With that same vaunted name, Virginity.
    Beauty is Nature's coin; must not be hoarded,
    But must be current; and the good thereof   740
    Consists in mutual and partaken bliss,
    Unsavoury in the enjoyment of itself.
    If you let slip time, like a neglected rose
    It withers on the stalk with languished head.
    Beauty is Nature's brag, and must be shown
    In courts, at feasts, and high solemnities,
    Where most may wonder at the workmanship.
    It is for homely features to keep home;
    They had their name thence: coarse complexions
    And cheeks of sorry grain will serve to ply   750
    The sampler, and to tease the huswife's wool.
    What need of vermeil-tinctured lip for that,
    Love-darting eyes, or tresses like the morn?
    There was another meaning in these gifts;
    Think what, and be advised; you are but young yet.

Lady. I had not thought to have unlocked my lips
    In this unhallowed air, but that this juggler
    Would think to charm my judgment, as mine eyes,
    Obtruding false rules pranked in reason's garb.
    I hate when vice can bolt her arguments   760
    And virtue has no tongue to check her pride.
    Impostor! do not charge most innocent Nature,
    As if she would her children should be riotous
    With her abundance. She, good cateress,
    Means her provision only to the good,
    That live according to her sober laws,
    And holy dictate of spare Temperance.
    If every just man that now pines with want
    Had but a moderate and beseeming share

Of that which lewdly-pampered Luxury 770
Now heaps upon some few with vast excess,
Nature's full blessings would be well dispensed
In unsuperfluous even proportions,
And she no whit encumbered with her store;
And then the Giver would be better thanked,
His praise due paid: for swinish gluttony
Ne'er looks to Heaven amidst his gorgeous feast,
But with besotted base ingratitude
Crams, and blasphemes his Feeder. Shall I go on?
Or have I said enow? To him that dares 780
Arm his profane tongue with contemptuous words
Against the sun-clad power of chastity
Fain would I something say;—yet to what end?
Thou hast nor ear, nor soul, to apprehend
The sublime notion and high mystery
That must be uttered to unfold the sage
And serious doctrine of Virginity;
And thou art worthy that thou shouldst not know
More happiness than this thy present lot.
Enjoy your dear wit, and gay rhetoric, 790
That hath so well been taught her dazzling fence;
Thou art not fit to hear thyself convinced.
Yet, should I try, the uncontrollèd worth
Of this pure cause would kindle my rapt spirits
To such a flame of sacred vehemence
That dumb things would be moved to sympathise,
And the brute Earth would lend her nerves, and shake,
Till all thy magic structures, reared so high,
Were shattered into heaps o'er thy false head.

Comus. She fables not. I feel that I do fear 800
Her words set off by some superior power;
And, though not mortal, yet a cold shuddering dew
Dips me all o'er, as when the wrath of Jove
Speaks thunder and the chains of Erebus
To some of Saturn's crew. I must dissemble,
And try her yet more strongly.—Come, no more!
This is mere moral babble, and direct

Against the canon laws of our foundation.
I must not suffer this; yet 'tis but the lees
And settlings of a melancholy blood.   810
But this will cure all straight; one sip of this
Will bathe the drooping spirits in delight
Beyond the bliss of dreams. Be wise, and taste.

The BROTHERS *rush in with swords drawn, wrest his glass out of his hand, and break it against the ground: his rout make sign of resistance, but are all driven in. The* ATTENDANT SPIRIT *comes in.*

Spirit. What! have you let the false enchanter scape?
    O ye mistook; ye should have snatched his wand,
And bound him fast. Without his rod reversed,
And backward mutters of dissevering power,
We cannot free the Lady that sits here
In stony fetters fixed and motionless.
Yet stay: be not disturbed; now I bethink me,   820
Some other means I have which may be used,
Which once of Meliboeus old I learnt,
The soothest shepherd that e'er piped on plains.

    There is a gentle nymph not far from hence,
That with moist curb sways the smooth Severn stream:
Sabrina is her name: a virgin pure;
Whilom she was the daughter of Locrine,
That had the sceptre from his father Brute.
She, guiltless damsel, flying the mad pursuit
Of her enragéd stepdame, Guendolen,   830
Commended her fair innocence to the flood
That stayed her flight with his cross-flowing course.
The water-nymphs, that in the bottom played,
Held up their pearled wrists, and took her in,
Bearing her straight to aged Nereus' hall;
Who, piteous of her woes, reared her lank head,
And gave her to his daughters to imbathe
In nectared lavers strewed with asphodel,
And through the porch and inlet of each sense
Dropt in ambrosial oils, till she revived,   840
And underwent a quick immortal change,

Made Goddess of the river. Still she retains
Her maiden gentleness, and oft at eve
Visits the herds along the twilight meadows,
Helping all urchin blasts, and ill-luck signs
That the shrewd meddling elf delights to make,
Which she with precious vialed liquors heals:
For which the shepherds, at their festivals,
Carol her goodness loud in rustic lays,
And throw sweet garland wreaths into her stream   850
Of pansies, pinks, and gaudy daffodils.
And, as the old swain said, she can unlock
The clasping charm, and thaw the numbing spell,
If she be right invoked in warbled song;
For maidenhood she loves, and will be swift
To aid a virgin, such as was herself,
In hard-besetting need. This will I try,
And add the power of some adjuring verse.

Song.

   Sabrina fair,
      Listen where thou art sitting   860
   Under the glassy, cool, translucent wave,
      In twisted braids of lilies knitting
   The loose train of thy amber-dropping hair;
      Listen for dear honour's sake,
      Goddess of the silver lake,
         Listen and save!

   Listen, and appear to us,
In name of great Oceanus.
By the earth-shaking Neptune's mace,
And Tethys' grave majestic pace;   870
By hoary Nereus' wrinkled look,
And the Carpathian wizard's hook;
By scaly Triton's winding shell,
And old soothsaying Glaucus' spell;
By Leucothea's lovely hands,
And her son that rules the strands;
By Thetis' tinsel-slippered feet,

> And the songs of Sirens sweet;
> By dead Parthenope's dear tomb,
> And fair Ligea's golden comb, 880
> Wherewith she sits on diamond rocks
> Sleeking her soft alluring locks;
> By all the Nymphs that nightly dance
> Upon thy streams with wily glance;
> Rise, rise, and heave thy rosy head
> From thy coral-paven bed,
> And bridle in thy headlong wave,
> Till thou our summons answered have.
>   Listen and save!

SABRINA *rises, attended by Water-nymphs, and sings.*

> By the rushy-fringéd bank, 890
> Where grows the willow and the osier dank,
>   My sliding chariot stays,
> Thick set with agate, and the azurn sheen
> Of turkis blue, and emerald green,
>   That in the channel strays;
> Whilst from off the waters fleet
> Thus I set my printless feet
> O'er the cowslip's velvet head,
>   That bends not as I tread.
> Gentle swain, at thy request 900
>   I am here!

Spirit. Goddess dear,
> We implore thy powerful hand
> To undo the charméd band
> Of true virgin here distressed
> Through the force and through the wile
> Of unblessed enchanter vile.

Sabrina. Shepherd, 'tis my office best
> To help ensnared chastity.
> Brightest Lady, look on me. 910
> Thus I sprinkle on thy breast
> Drops that from my fountain pure

    I have kept of precious cure;
    Thrice upon thy finger's tip,
    Thrice upon thy rubied lip:
    Next this marble venomed seat,
    Smeared with gums of glutinous heat,
    I touch with chaste palms moist and cold.
    Now the spell hath lost his hold;
    And I must haste ere morning hour   920
    To wait in Amphitrite's bower.

    Sabrina descends, and the LADY rises out of her seat.

Spirit. Virgin, daughter of Locrine,
    Sprung of old Anchises' line,
    May thy brimmèd waves for this
    Their full tribute never miss
    From a thousand petty rills,
    That tumble down the snowy hills:
    Summer drouth or singèd air
    Never scorch thy tresses fair,
    Nor wet October's torrent flood   930
    Thy molten crystal fill with mud;
    May thy billows roll ashore
    The beryl and the golden ore;
    May thy lofty head be crowned
    With many a tower and terrace round,
    And here and there thy banks upon
    With groves of myrrh and cinnamon.
    Come, Lady; while Heaven lends us grace,
    Let us fly this cursèd place,
    Lest the sorcerer us entice   940
    With some other new device.
    Not a waste or needless sound
    Till we come to holier ground.
    I shall be your faithful guide
    Through this gloomy covert wide;
    And not many furlongs thence
    Is your Father's residence,
    Where this night are met in state

Many a friend to gratulate
　　　His wished presence, and beside　　　　　　　　　　950
　　　All the swains that there abide
　　　With jigs and rural dance resort.
　　　We shall catch them at their sport,
　　　And our sudden coming there
　　　Will double all their mirth and cheer.
　　　Come, let us haste; the stars grow high,
　　　But Night sits monarch yet in the mid sky.

The Scene changes, presenting Ludlow Town, and the President's Castle; then come in Country Dancers; after them the ATTENDANT SPIRIT, *with the Two* BROTHERS *and the* LADY.

Song.

Spirit. Back, shepherds, back! Enough your play
　　　Till next sunshine holiday.
　　　Here be, without duck or nod,　　　　　　　　　　960
　　　Other trippings to be trod
　　　Of lighter toes, and such court guise
　　　As Mercury did first devise
　　　With the mincing Dryades
　　　On the lawns and on the leas.

This second Song presents them to their Father and Mother.
　　　Noble Lord and Lady bright,
　　　I have brought ye new delight.
　　　Here behold so goodly grown
　　　Three fair branches of your own.
　　　Heaven hath timely tried their youth,　　　　　　　970
　　　Their faith, their patience, and their truth,
　　　And sent them here through hard assays
　　　With a crown of deathless praise,
　　　To triumph in victorious dance
　　　O'er sensual folly and intemperance.
　　　The dances ended, the SPIRIT epiloguizes.

Spirit. To the ocean now I fly,
　　　And those happy climes that lie

Where day never shuts his eye,
Up in the broad fields of the sky.
There I suck the liquid air, 980
All amidst the gardens fair
Of Hesperus, and his daughters three
That sing about the golden tree.
Along the crispéd shades and bowers
Revels the spruce and jocund Spring;
The Graces and the rosy-bosomed Hours
Thither all their bounties bring.
There eternal Summer dwells,
And west winds with musky wing
About the cedarn alleys fling 990
Nard and cassia's balmy smells.
Iris there with humid bow
Waters the odorous banks, that blow
Flowers of more mingled hue
Than her purfled scarf can shew,
And drenches with Elysian dew
(List, mortals, if your ears be true)
Beds of hyacinth and roses,
Where young Adonis oft reposes,
Waxing well of his deep wound, 1000
In slumber soft, and on the ground
Sadly sits the Assyrian queen.
But far above, in spangled sheen,
Celestial Cupid, her famed son, advanced
Holds his dear Psyche, sweet entranced
After her wandering labours long,
Till free consent the gods among
Make her his eternal bride,
And from her fair unspotted side
Two blissful twins are to be born, 1010
Youth and Joy; so Jove hath sworn.
But now my task is smoothly done,
I can fly, or I can run
Quickly to the green earth's end,
Where the bowed welkin slow doth bend,
And from thence can soar as soon

To the corners of the moon.
Mortals, that would follow me,
Love Virtue; she alone is free.
She can teach ye how to climb   1020
Higher than the sphery chime;
Or, if Virtue feeble were,
Heaven itself would stoop to her.

NOTES.

discovers, exhibits, displays. The usual sense of 'discover' is to find out or make known, but in Milton and Shakespeare the prefix *dis-* has often the more purely negative force of *un-*: hence discover = uncover, reveal. Comp.—

> "Some high-climbing hill
> Which to his eye *discovers* unaware
> The goodly prospect of some foreign land."
> *Par. Lost*, iii. 546.

Attendant Spirit descends. The part of the attendant spirit was taken by Lawes (see Introduction), who, in his prologue or opening speech, explains who he is and on what errand he has been sent, hints at the plot of the whole masque, and at the same time compliments the Earl in whose honour the masque is being given (lines 30-36). In the ancient classical drama the prologue was sometimes an outline of the plot, sometimes an address to the audience, and sometimes introductory to the plot. The opening of *Comus* prepares the audience and also directly addresses it (line 43). For the form of the epilogue in the actual performance of the masque see note, l. 975-6.

1. starry threshold, etc. Comp. Virgil: "The sire of gods and monarch of men summons a council to the starry chamber" *(sideream in sedem)*, *Aen.* x. 2.
2. mansion, abode. Trench points out that this word denotes strictly "a place of tarrying," which might be for a longer or a shorter time: hence 'a resting-place.' Comp. *John*, xiv. 2, "In my Father's house are many *mansions*"; and *Il Pens.* 93, "Her *mansion* in this

fleshly nook." The word has now lost the notion of tarrying, and is applied to a large and important dwelling-house. **where, in which**: the antecedent is separated from the relative, a frequent construction in Milton (comp. lines 66, 821, etc.). So in Latin, where the grammatical connection would generally be sufficiently indicated by the inflection. **shapes ... spirits.** An instance of the manner in which Milton endows spiritual beings with personality without making them too distinct. "Of all the poets who have introduced into their works the agency of supernatural beings Milton has succeeded best" (Macaulay). We see this in *Par. Lost (e.g.* ii. 666). Compare the use of the word 'shape' (Lat. *umbra*) in l. 207: also *L'Alleg.* 4, "horrid *shapes* and shrieks"; and *Il Pens.* 6, "fancies fond with gaudy *shapes* possess." Milton's use of the demonstrative those in this line is noteworthy; comp. *"that* last infirmity of noble mind," *Lyc.* 71: it implies that the reference is to something well known, and that further particularisation is needless.

3. **insphered.** 'Sphere,' with its derivatives 'sphery,' 'insphere,' and 'unsphere' *(Il Pens.* 88), is used by Milton with a literal reference to the cosmical framework as a whole (see *Hymn Nat.* 48) or to some portion of it. In Shakespeare 'sphere' occurs in the wider sense of 'the path in which anything moves,' and it is to this metaphorical use of the word that we owe such phrases as 'a person's sphere of life,' 'sphere of action,' etc. See also *Comus*, 112-4, 241-3, 1021; *Arc.* 62-7; *Par. Lost*, v. 618; where there are references to the music of the spheres.

4. **mild**: an attributive of the whole clause, 'regions of calm and serene air.' **calm and serene.** These are not mere synonyms: the Lat. *serenus* = bright or unclouded, so that the two epithets are to be respectively contrasted with 'smoke' and 'stir' (line 5); 'calm' being opposed to 'stir' and 'serene' to 'smoke.' Compare Homer's description of the seat of the gods: "Not by wind is it shaken, nor ever wet with rain, nor doth the snow come nigh thereto, but *most clear* air is spread about it *cloudless,* and the white light floats over it," *Odyssey*, vi.: comp. note, l. 977.

5. **this dim spot.** The Spirit describes the Earth as it appears to those immortal shapes whose presence he has just quitted.

6. There are here two attributive clauses: "which men call Earth" and "(in which) men strive," etc. **low-thoughted care**; narrow-

minded anxiety, care about earthly things. Comp. the form of the adjective 'low-browed,' *L'Alleg.* 8: both epithets are borrowed by Pope in his *Eloisa.*

7. This line is attributive to 'men.' pestered . . . pinfold, crowded together in this cramped space, the Earth. *Pester*, which has no connection with *pest*, is a shortened form of *impester*, Fr. *empêtrer*, to shackle a horse by the foot when it is at pasture. The radical sense is that of clogging (comp. *Son.* xii. 1); hence of crowding; and finally of annoyance or encumbrance of any kind. 'Pinfold' is strictly an enclosure in which stray cattle are *pounded* or shut up: etymologically, the word = *pind-fold*, a corruption of *pound-fold*. Comp. *impound*, sheep-*fold*, etc.

8. frail and feverish. Comp. "life's fitful fever" *(Macbeth*, iii. 2. 23). This line, like several of the adjacent ones, is alliterative.

9. crown that Virtue gives. This is Scriptural language: comp. *Rev.* iv. 4; 2 *Tim.* iv. 8, "Henceforth there is laid up for me the crown of righteousness."

10. this mortal change. In Milton's MS. line 7 was followed by the words, 'beyond the written date of mortal change,' *i.e.* beyond, or after, man's appointed time to die. These words were struck out, but we may suppose that the words 'mortal change' in line 10 have a similar meaning. Milton frequently uses 'mortal' in the sense of 'liable to death,' and hence 'human' as opposed to 'divine': the mortal change is therefore 'the change which occurs to all human beings.' Comp. *Job*, xiv. 14: "all the days of my appointed time will I wait, till my *change* come": see also line 841. Prof. Masson takes it to mean 'this mortal state of life,' as distinguished from a future state of immortality. The Spirit uses 'this' as in line 8, in contrast with 'those,' line 2.

11. enthroned gods, etc. In allusion to *Rev.* iv. 4, "And upon the thrones I saw four and twenty elders sitting, arrayed in white garments; and on their heads crowns of gold." Milton frequently speaks of the inhabitants of heaven as *enthroned.* The accent here falls on the first syllable of the word.

12. Yet some there be, etc.: 'Although men are generally so exclusively occupied with the cares of this life, there are nevertheless a few who aspire,' etc. *Be* is here purely indicative. This usage is frequent in Elizabethan English, and still survives in parts of England. Comp. *Lines on Univ. Carrier*,

ii. 25, where it occurs in a similar phrase, "there be that say 't'": also lines 519, 668. It is employed to refer to a number of persons or things, regarded as a class. **by due steps**, *i.e.* by the steps that are due or appointed: comp. *'due* feet,' *Il Pens.* 155. *Due*, *duty*, and *debt* are all from Lat. *debitus*, owed.

13. **their just hands.** 'Just' belongs to the predicate: 'to lay their just hands' = to lay their hands with justice. **golden key.** Comp. *Matt.* xvi. 19, "I will give unto thee the *keys* of the kingdom of heaven"; also *Lyc.* 111:

> "Two massy keys he bore of metals twain
> (The *golden* opes, the iron shuts amain)."

15. **errand:** comp. *Par. Lost*, iii. 652, "One of the seven Who in God's presence, nearest to his throne, Stand ready at command, and are his eyes That run through all the Heavens, or down to the Earth Bear his swift *errands*": also vii. 579. **but for such**, *i.e.* unless it were for such.

16. 'I would not sully the purity of my heavenly garments with the noisome vapour of this sin-corrupted earth.' **ambrosial**, heavenly; also used by Milton in the sense of 'conferring immortality': comp. l. 840; *Par. Lost*, ii. 245; iv. 219, "blooming *ambrosial* fruit." 'Ambrosial,' like 'amaranthus' *(Lyc.* 149), is cognate with the Sanskrit *amríta*, undying; and is applied by Homer to the hair of the gods: similarly in Tennyson's *Oenone*, 174: see also *In Memoriam*, lxxxvi. Ben Jonson *(Neptune's Triumph)* has 'ambrosian hands,' *i.e.* hands fit for a deity. Ambrosia was the food of the gods. **weeds**: now used chiefly in the phrase "widow's weeds," *i.e.* mourning garment. Milton and Shakespeare use it in the general sense of garment or covering: in the lines *On the Death of a Fair Infant*, it is applied to the human body itself; comp. also *M. N. D.* ii. 1. 255, *"Weed* wide enough to wrap a fairy in." See also *Comus*, 189, 390.

18. **But to my task**, *i.e.* but I must proceed to my task: see l. 1012.

19. **every ... each.** It is usual to write *every ... every*, or *each ... each*, but Milton occasionally uses 'every' and 'each' together: comp. l. 311 and *Lyc.* 93, *"every* gust ... off *each* beaked promontory." *Every* denotes each without exception, and can now only be

used with reference to more than two objects; *each* may refer to two or more.

20. by lot, etc. When Saturn (Kronos) was dethroned, his empire of the universe was distributed amongst his three sons, Jupiter ('high' Jove), Neptune (the god of the Sea), and Pluto ('nether' or Stygian Jove). In *Iliad* xv. Neptune (Poseidon) says: "For three brethren are we, and sons of Kronos, whom Rhea bare ... And in three lots are all things divided, and each drew a domain of his own, and to me fell the hoary sea, to be my habitation for ever, when we shook the lots." nether, lower: comp. the phrase 'the upper and the nether lip,' and the name Netherlands. Hell, the abode of Pluto, is called by Milton 'the nether empire' *(Par. Lost*, ii. 295). The form *nethermost (Par. Lost*, ii. 955) is, like *aftermost* and *foremost*, a double superlative.

21. sea-girt isles. Ben Jonson calls Britain a 'sea-girt isle': comp. l. 27. *Isle* is the M.E. *ile*, in which form the *s* has been dropped: it is from O.F. *isle*, Lat. *insula*. It is therefore distinct from *island*, where an *s* has, by confusion, been inserted. Island = M.E. *iland*, A.S. *igland (ig* = island: *land* = land). In line 50 Milton wrote 'iland.'

22. like to rich and various gems, etc. Shakespeare describes England as a 'precious stone set in the silver sea,' *Richard II*. ii. 1. 46: he also speaks of Heaven as being *inlayed* with stars, *Cym*. v. 5. 352; *M. of V*. v. 1. 59, "Look how the floor of heaven Is thick *inlaid* with patines of bright gold." Compare also *Par. Lost*, iv. 700, where Milton refers to the ground as having a rich *inlay* of flowers. But for its inlay of islands the sea would be bare or unadorned. like: here followed by the preposition *to*, and having its proper force as an adjective: comp. *Il Pens*. 9. Whether *like* is used as an adjective or an adverb, the preposition is now usually omitted: comp. l. 57.

24. to grace, *i.e.* to show favour to: a clause of purpose.

25. By course commits, etc., *i.e.* "In regular distribution he commits to each his distinct government." several: separate or distinct. Radically *several* is from the verb *sever*: it is now used only with plural nouns.

26. sapphire. This colour is again associated with the sea in line 29: see note there.

27. little tridents, in contrast with that of Neptune, who, "with his trident touched the stars" *(Neptune's Triumph, Proteus' Song*, Ben Jonson).
28. greatest and the best. Comp. Shakespeare's eulogy in *Rich. II.* ii. 1: also Ben Jonson's "Albion, Prince of all his Isles," *Neptune's Triumph, Apollo's Song.*
29. quarters, divides into distinct regions. Comp. Dryden, *Georg. I.* 208:

> "Sailors *quarter'd* Heaven, and found a name
> For every fixt and ev'ry wandering star."

Some would take the word as strictly denoting division into *four* parts: "at that time the island was actually divided into four separate governments: for besides those at London and Edinburgh, there were Lords President of the North and of Wales." (Keightley). blue-haired deities. These must be distinct from the tributary gods who wield their little tridents (line 27), otherwise the thought would ill accord with the complimentary nature of lines 30-36. Regarding the epithet 'blue-haired' Masson asks: "Can there be a recollection of blue as the British colour, inherited from the old times of blue-stained Britons who fought with Caesar? Green-haired is the usual epithet for Neptune and his subordinates": in Spenser, for example, the sea-nymphs have long green hair. But Ovid expressly calls the sea-deities *caerulei dii*, and Neptune *caeruleus deus*, thus associating blue with the sea.

30. 'And all this region that looks towards the West *(i.e.* Wales) is entrusted to a noble peer of great integrity and power.' The peer referred to is the Earl of Bridgewater. As Lord President he was entrusted with the civil and military administration of Wales and the four English counties of Gloucester, Worcester, Hereford, and Shropshire. That he was a nobleman of high character is shown by the fact that from 1617, when he was nominated one of "his Majestie's Counsellors," he had continued to serve in various important public and private offices. On his monument there is the following: "He was a profound Scholar, an able Statesman, and a good Christian: he was a dutiful Son to his Mother the Church of England

in her persecution, as well as in her great splendour; a loyal Subject to his Sovereign in those worst of times, when it was accounted treason not to be a traitor. As he lived 70 years a pattern of virtue, so he died an example of patience and piety." falling sun: Lat. *sol occidens*. Orient and occident (lit. 'rising' and 'falling') are frequently used to denote the East and the West.

31. mickle (A.S. *micel*) great. From this word comes *much*. 'Mickle' and 'muckle' are current in Scotland in the sense of great. Comp. *Rom. and Jul.* ii. 3. 15, "O, *mickle* is the powerful grace that lies In herbs," etc.

33. An old and haughty nation. The Welsh are Kelts, an Aryan people who probably first entered Britain about B.C. 500: they are therefore rightly spoken of as an old nation. Compare Ben Jonson's piece *For the Honour of Wales*:

> "I is not come here to taulk of Brut,
> From whence the Welse does take his root," etc.

That they were haughty and 'proud in arms' the Romans found, and after them the Saxons: the latter never really held more than the counties of Monmouth and Hereford. In the reign of Edward I. attempts were made by that king to induce the Welsh to come to terms, but the answer of the Barons was: "We dare not submit to Edward, nor will we suffer our prince to do so, nor do homage to strangers, whose tongue, ways and laws we know not of: we have only raised war in defence of our lands, laws and rights." By a statute of Henry VIII. this 'haughty' people were put in possession of the same rights and liberties as the English. proud in arms: this is Virgil's *belloque superbum*, *Aen.* i. 21 (Warton).

34. nursed in princely lore, brought up in a manner worthy of their high position. It is to be noted that the Bridgewater family was by birth distantly connected with the royal family. Milton may allude merely to their connection with the court. *Lore* is cognate with *learn*.

35. their father's state. This probably refers to the actual ceremonies connected with the installation of the Earl as Lord President. The old sense of 'state' is 'chair of state': comp. *Arc.* 81, and

Jonson's *Hymenaei*, "And see where Juno ... Displays her glittering *state and chair.*"

36. new-intrusted, an adjective compounded of a participle and a simple adverb, *new* being = newly; comp. 'smooth-dittied,' l. 86. Contrast the form of the epithet "blue-haired," where the compound adjective is formed as if from a noun, "blue-hair": comp. "rushy-fringed," l. 890. Strictly speaking, the Earl's power was not 'new-intrusted,' though it was newly assumed. See Introduction.

37. perplexed, interwoven, entangled (Lat. *plecto*, to plait or twist). The word is here used literally and is therefore applicable to inanimate objects. The accent is on the first syllable.

38. horror. This word is meant not merely to indicate terror, but also to describe the appearance of the paths. Horror is from Lat. *horrere*, to bristle, and may be rendered 'shagginess' or 'ruggedness,' just as *horrid*, l. 429, means bristling or rugged. Comp. *Par. Lost*, i. 563, "a *horrid* front Of dreadful length, and dazzling arms." shady brows: this may refer to the trees and bushes overhanging the paths, as the brow overhangs the eyes.

39. Threats: not current as a verb. forlorn, now used only as an adjective, is the past participle of the old verb *forleosen*, to lose utterly: the prefix *for* has an intensive force, as in *forswear*; but in the latter word the sense of *from* is more fully preserved in the prefix. See note, l. 234.

40. tender age. Lady Alice Egerton was about fourteen years of age; the two brothers were younger than she.

41. But that, etc. Grammatically, *but* may be regarded as a subordinative conjunction = 'unless (it had happened) that I was despatched': or, taking it in its original prepositional sense, we may regard it as governing the substantive clause, 'that ... guard.' quick command: the adjective has the force of an adverb, quick commands being commands that are to be carried quickly. sovran, supreme. This is Milton's spelling of the modern word *sovereign*, in which the *g* is due to the mistaken notion that the last syllable of the word is cognate with *reign*. The word is from Lat. *superanum* = chief: comp. l. 639.

43. And listen why; *sc.* 'I was despatched.' The language of lines 43, 44 is suggested by Horace's *Odes*, iii. 1, 2: "Favete linguis;

carmina non prius Audita ... canto." The poet implies that the plot of his mask is original: it is not (he says) to be found in any ancient or modern song or tale that was ever recited either in the 'hall' (= banqueting-hall) or in the 'bower' (= private chamber). Or 'hall' and 'bower' may denote respectively the room of the lord and that of his lady.

46. Milton in his usual significant manner (comp. *L'Allegro* and *Il Penseroso*), proceeds to invent a genealogy for Comus. The mask is designed to celebrate the victory of Purity and Reason over Desire and Enchantment. Comus, who represents the latter, must therefore spring from parents representing the pleasure of man's lower nature and the misuse of man's higher powers on behalf of falsehood and impurity. These parents are the wine-god Bacchus and the sorceress Circe. The former, mated with Love, is the father of Mirth (see *L'Allegro*); but, mated with the cunning Circe, his offspring is a voluptuary whose gay exterior and flattering speech hide his dangerously seductive and magical powers. He bears no resemblance, therefore, to Comus as represented in Ben Jonson's *Pleasure reconciled to Virtue*, in which mask "Comus" and "The Belly" are throughout synonymous. In the *Agamemnon* of Aeschylus, Comus is a "drinker of human blood"; in Philostratus, he is a rose-crowned wine-bibber; in Dekker he is "the clerk of gluttony's kitchen"; in Massinger he is "the god of pleasure"; and in the work of Erycius Puteanus he is a graceful reveller, the genius of love and cheerfulness. Prof. Masson says, "Milton's *Comus* is a creation of his own, for which he was as little indebted intrinsically to Puteanus as to Ben Jonson. For the purpose of his masque at Ludlow Castle he was bold enough to add a brand-new god, no less, to the classic Pantheon, and to import him into Britain." Bacchus, the god who taught men the preparation of wine. He is the Greek Dionysus, who, on one of his voyages, hired a vessel belonging to some Tyrrhenian pirates: these men resolved to sell him as a slave. Thereupon, he changed the mast and oars of the ship into serpents and the sailors into dolphins. The meeting of Bacchus with Circe is Milton's own invention; in the *Odyssey* it is Ulysses who lights upon her island: "And we came to the isle Ææan, where dwelt Circe of the braided tresses, an awful

goddess of mortal speech, own sister to the wizard Æetes," *Odys.* x. from out, etc. Comp. *Par. Lost*, v. 345. 'From out' has the same force as the more common 'out from.'

47. misusèd, abused. The prefix *mis*-was very generally used by Milton; *e.g. mislike, misdeem, miscreated, misthought* (all obsolete).

48. After the Tuscan mariners transformed, *i.e.* after the transformation of the Tuscan mariners (see Ovid, *Met.* iii.). They are called Tuscan, because Tyrrhenia in Central Italy was named Etruria or Tuscia by the Romans: Etruria includes modern Tuscany. This grammatical construction is common in Latin; a passive participle combined with a substantive answering to an English verbal or abstract noun connected with another noun by the preposition *of*, and used to denote a fact in the past; *e.g.* "since created man" *(P. L.* i. 573) = since the creation of man: "this loss recovered" *(P. L.* ii. 21) = the recovery of this loss.

49. as the winds listed; at the pleasure of the winds: comp. *John*, iii. 8, "the wind bloweth where it *listeth*"; *Lyc.* 123. The verb *list* is, in older English, generally used impersonally, and in Chaucer we find 'if thee lust' or 'if thee list' = if it please thee. The word survives in the adjective *listless* of which the older form was *lustless*: the noun *lust* has lost its original and wider sense (which it still has in German), and now signifies 'longing desire.'

50. On Circe's island fell. Circe's island = Aeaea, off the coast of Latium. Circe was the daughter of Helios (the Sun) by the ocean-nymph Perse. On 'island,' see note, l. 21; and with this use of the verb *fall* comp. the Latin *incidere in.* The sudden introduction of the interrogative clause in this line is an example of the figure of speech called anadiplosis.

51. charmèd cup, *i.e.* liquor that has been *charmed* or rendered magical. *Charms* are incantations or magic verses (Lat. *carmina*): comp. lines 526 and 817. Grammatically, 'cup' is the object of 'tasted.'

52. Whoever tasted lost, *i.e.* who tasted (he) lost. In this construction *whoever* must precede both verbs; Shakespeare frequently uses *who* in this sense, and Milton occasionally: comp. *Son.* xii. 12, "*who* loves that must first be wise and good." See Abbott, § 251. lost his upright shape. In *Odyssey* x. we read: "So Circe led them (followers of Ulysses) in and set them upon chairs and

high seats, and made them a mess of cheese and barley-meal and yellow honey with Pramnian wine, and mixed harmful drugs with the food to make them utterly forget their own country. Now when she had given them the cup and they had drunk it off, presently she smote them with a wand, and in the styes of the swine she penned them. So they had the head and voice, the bristles and the shape of swine, but their mind abode even as of old. Thus were they penned there weeping, and Circe flung them acorns and mast and fruit of the cornel tree to eat, whereon wallowing swine do always batten." *(Butcher and Lang's translation.)*

54. clustering locks: comp. l. 608. Milton here pictures the Theban Bacchus, a type of manly beauty, having his head crowned with a wreath of vine and ivy: both of these plants were sacred to the god. Comp. *L'Alleg.* 16, "ivy-crowned Bacchus"; *Par. Lost*, iv. 303; *Sams. Agon.* 569.

55. his blithe youth, *i.e.* his fresh young figure.

57. 'A son much like his father, but more like his mother.' This may indicate that it is upon Comus's character as a sorcerer rather than as a reveller that the story of the mask depends. Comp. *Masque of Hymen*:

> "Much of the father's face,
> More of the mother's grace."

58. Comus: see note, l. 46. The Greek word κῶμος denoted a revel or merry-making; afterwards it came to mean the personification of riotous mirth, the god of Revel. Hence also the word *comedy*. In classical mythology the individuality of Comus is not well defined: this enabled Milton more readily to endow him with entirely new characteristics.

59. frolic: an instance of the original use of the word as an adjective; comp. *L'Alleg.* 18, "frolic wind"; Tennyson's *Ulysses*, "a frolic welcome." It is now chiefly used as a noun or a verb, and a new adjective, *frolicsome*, has taken its place; from this, again, comes the noun *frolicsomeness*. *Frolic* is from the Dutch, and cognate with German *fröhlich*, so that *lic* in 'frolic' corresponds to *ly* in such words as cleanly, godly, etc. of: this use of the preposition

may be compared with the Latin genitive in such phrases as *æger animi* = sick of soul; of = 'because of' or 'in respect of.'

60. Roving the Celtic and Iberian fields, *i.e.* roving through Gaul and Spain. 'Rove' here governs an accusative: comp. *Lyc.* 173, "walked the waves"; *Par. Lost*, i. 521, "roamed the utmost Isles."

61. betakes him. The pronoun has here a reflective force: in Elizabethan English, and still more often in Early English, this use of the simple pronouns is common (see Abbott, § 223). Compare l. 163. ominous; literally = full of omens or portents: comp. 'monstrous' = full of monsters *(Lyc.* 158); also l. 79. 'Ominous' has now acquired the sense of 'ill-omened'; compare the acquired sense of 'hapless,' 'unfortunate,' etc.

65. orient, bright. The Lat. *oriens* = rising; hence (from being applied to the sun) = eastern (l. 30); and hence generally 'bright' or 'shining': comp. *Par. Lost*, i. 546, "With *orient* colours waving."

66. drouth of Phoebus, *i.e.* thirst caused by the heat of the sun. Phoebus is Apollo, the Sun-god. Compare l. 928, where 'drouth' = want of rain; the more usual spelling is *drought*. which: see note, l. 2. 'Which' is here object of 'taste,' and refers to 'liquor.'

67. fond, foolish (its primary sense). *Fonned* was the participle of an old verb *fonnen*, to be foolish. The word is now used to express great liking or affection: the idea of folly being almost entirely lost. Chaucer has *fonne*, a fool: comp. *Il Pens.* 6, "fancies *fond*"; *Lyc.* 56, "I *fondly* dream"; *Sams. Agon.* 1682, "So *fond* are mortal men."

68. Soon as, etc., *i.e.* as soon as the magical draught produces its effect. In line 66 *as* is temporal. potion. Radically, potion = a drink, but it is generally used in the sense of a medicated or poisonous draught. *Poison* is the same word through the French.

69. Express resemblance of the gods. Comp. Shakespeare: "What a piece of work is man! ... in action how like an angel, in apprehension, how like a god!" See also *Par. Lost*, iii. 44, "human face divine."

71. ounce. This is the *Felis uncia*, allied to the panther and the cheetah. Some connect it with the Persian *yúz*, panther.

72. All other parts, etc. In the *Odyssey* (see note on l. 52) the bodies of those transformed by Circe were entirely changed; here only the head. As one editor observes, this suited the convenience of the performers who were to appear on the stage in masks (see *Stage direction*, l. 92-3). Grammatically, line 72 is an example of the absolute construction, common in Latin. The noun ('parts') is neither the subject nor the object of a verb, but is used along with some attributive adjunct—generally a participle ('remaining')—to serve the purpose of an adverb or adverbial clause. The noun (or pronoun) is usually said to be the nominative absolute; but, in the case of pronouns, Milton uses the nominative and the objective indifferently. In Old English the dative was used.

73. perfect, complete (Lat. *perfectus*, done thoroughly).

74. Not once perceive, etc. This was not the case with the followers of Ulysses: see note, l. 52.

76. friends and native home forgot. Circe's cup has here the effect ascribed to the lotus in *Odyssey* ix. "Now whosoever of them did eat the honey-sweet fruit of the lotus had no more wish to bring tidings nor to come back, but there he chose to abide with the lotus-eating men, ever feeding on the lotus and forgetful of his homeward way." In Tennyson's *Lotos-Eaters* there is no forgetfulness of friends and home: "Sweet it was to dream of Fatherland, Of child, and wife and slave." Masson also refers to Plato's ethical application of the story *(Rep.* viii.); "Plato speaks of the moral lotophagus, or youth steeped in sensuality, as accounting his very viciousness a developed manhood, and the so-called virtues but signs of rusticity." Compare also Spenser, *F. Q.* ii. 12. 86, "One above the rest in speciall, That had an hog been late, . . . did him miscall, That had from hoggish form him brought to natural."

77. sensual sty: see note on l. 52. To those who, "with low-thoughted care," are "unmindful of the crown that Virtue gives," the world becomes little better than a sensual sty. This line is adverbial to *forget*.

78. favoured: compare Lat. *gratus* = favoured (adj.).

79. adventurous, full of risks. The current sense of 'adventurous,' applied only to persons, is "enterprising." See l. 61, 609. glade: strictly, an open space in a wood, and hence applied (as here)

to the wood itself. It is cognate with *glow* and *glitter*, and its fundamental sense is 'a passage for light' (Skeat).

80. glancing star, a shooting star. Comp. *Par. Lost*, iv. 556:
> "Swift as a shooting star
> In autumn thwarts the night."

The rhythm of the line and the prevalence of sibilants suit the sense.

81. convoy: comp. *Par. Lost*, vi. 752, *"convoyed* By four cherubic shapes." It is another form of *convey* (Lat. *con* = together, *via* = a way).

83. sky-robes: the "ambrosial weeds" of line 16. Iris' woof, material dyed in rainbow colours. The goddess Iris was a personification of the rainbow: comp. l. 992 and *Par. Lost*, xi. 244, "Iris had dipped the woof." Etymologically, *woof* is connected with *web* and *weave*: it is short for *on-wef* = on-web, *i.e.* the cross threads laid on the warp of a loom.

84. weeds: see note, l. 16.

86. That to the service, etc. The part of the Spirit was acted by Lawes, first in "sky-robes," then in shepherd dress. In the dedication of *Comus* by Lawes to Lord Brackley (anonymous edition of 1637), he alludes to the favours that had been shown him by the Bridgewater family. In the above lines Milton compliments Lawes and enables Lawes to compliment the Earl (see Introduction).

86. smooth-dittied: sweetly-worded. 'Ditty' (Lat. *dictatum*) strictly denotes the words of a song as distinct from the musical accompaniment; it is now applied to any little piece intended to be sung: comp. *Lyc.* 32. For a similar panegyric on Lawes' musical genius compare *Son.* xiii. The musical alliteration in lines 86-88 should be noted.

87. knows to still, etc.: comp. *Lyc.* 10, "he knew Himself to sing."

88. nor of less faith, etc.; *i.e.* he is not less faithful than he is skilful in music; and from the nature of his occupation he is most likely to be at hand should any emergency arise.

92. viewless, invisible: comp. *The Passion*, 50, *"viewless* wing"; *Par. Lost*, iii. 518. Masson calls this a peculiarly Shakespearian word: see *M. for M.* iii. 1. 124, "To be imprisoned in the viewless winds." The word is obsolete, but poets use great liberty in the

formation of adjectives in *-less*: comp. Shelley's *Sensitive Plant*, 'windless clouds.' See note, l. 574. charming-rod: see note, l. 52: also l. 653. rout, a disorderly crowd. The word is also used in the sense of 'defeat,' and is cognate with *route*, *rote*, and *rut*. All come from Lat. *ruptus*, broken: a 'rout' is the breaking up of a crowd, or a crowd broken up; a 'route' is a way broken through a forest; 'rote' is a beaten track; and a 'rut' is a track left by a wheel. See *Lyc.* 61, "by the *rout* that made the hideous roar."

93. star . . . fold, the evening star, Hesperus, an appellation of the planet Venus: comp. *Lyc.* 30. As the morning star (called by Shakespeare the 'unfolding star'), it is called Phosphorus or Lucifer, the light-bringer. Hence Tennyson's allusion:

> "Bright Phosphor, fresher for the night, . . .
> Sweet *Hesper-Phosphor*, double name."—
> *In Memoriam*, cxxi.

Lines 93-144 are in rhymed couplets, and consist for the most part of eight syllables each. The prevailing accentuation is iambic.

94. top of heaven, etc., *i.e.* is far above the horizon. So in *Lyc.* 31, it is said to slope "toward heaven's *descent*," *i.e.* to sink towards the horizon. Comp. Virgil, *Aen.* ii. 250, "Round rolls the sky, and on comes Night from the ocean."

95. gilded car: Apollo, as the god of the Sun, rode in a golden chariot. Comp. Chaucer, *Test. of Creseide*, 208, "Phoebus' golden cart"; and "Phoebus' wain," line 190.

96. his glowing axle doth allay. In the *Hymn of the Nativity* Milton alludes to the "burning axle-tree" of the sun: comp. *Aen.* iv. 482, "Atlas *Axem* umero torquet." There is here an allusion to the opinion of the ancients that the setting of the sun in the Atlantic Ocean was accompanied with a noise, as of the sea hissing (Todd). 'Allay' would thus denote 'quench' or 'cool.' *His*, in this line, = *its*. *Its* occurs only three times in Milton's poems, *Od. Nat.* 106; *Par. Lost*, i. 254; *Par. Lost*, iv. 813: the word is found also in Lawes' dedication of *Comus*. The word does not occur in English at all until the end of the sixteenth century, the possessive case of the neuter pronoun *it* and of

the masculine *he* being *his*. This gave rise to confusion when the old gender system decayed, and the form *its* gradually came into use, until, by the end of the seventeenth century, it was in general use. Milton, however, scarcely recognised it, its place in his involved syntax being taken by the relative pronouns and other connectives, or by *his, her, thereof,* etc.

97. steep Atlantic stream. To the ancients the Ocean was the great *stream* that encompassed the earth: *Iliad*, xiv., "the deep-flowing Okeanos (βαθύρροος)." With this use of 'steep' compare the phrase 'the high seas.'

98. slope sun, sun sunk beneath the horizon, so that the only rays visible shoot up into the sky. *Slope* = sloped; also used by Milton as an adverb = aslope *(Par. Lost*, iv. 591), and as a verb *(Lyc.* 31).

99. dusky. Milton first wrote 'northern.'

100. Pacing toward the other goal, etc. Comp. *Psalm* xix. 5: "The sun as a bridegroom cometh out of his chamber, and rejoiceth as a strong man to run a race."

102. The spirit of lines 102-144 may be contrasted with that of *L'Allegro*, 25-40. Both pieces are calls upon Mirth and Pleasure, and both are therefore suitably expressed in the same tripping measure and with many similarities of language. But the pleasures of *L'Allegro* begin with the sun-rise and yet are "unreproved"; those of *Comus* and his crew begin with the darkness and are "unreproved" only if "these dun shades will ne'er report" them. The "light fantastic toe" of the one is not the "tipsy dance" of the other; and the laughter and liberty that betoken the absence of "wrinkled Care" have nothing in common with the "midnight shout and revelry" that can be enjoyed only when Rigour, Advice, strict Age, and sour Severity have "gone to bed." The "quips and cranks" of *L'Allegro* have given way to the magic rites of *Comus*, and the wreathed smiles and dimples that adorn the face of innocent Mirth are ill replaced by the wine-dropping "rosy twine" of revelry.

104. jollity: has here its modern sense of boisterous mirth. In Milton occasionally the adjective 'jolly' (Fr. *joli*, pretty) has its primary sense of pleasing or festive.

105. Braid your locks with rosy twine; 'entwine your hair with wreaths of roses.'
106. dropping odours: comp. l. 862-3.
108. Advice ... scrupulous head. 'Advice,' now used chiefly to signify counsel given by another, was formerly used also of self-counsel or deliberation. See Chaucer, *Prologue*, 786, "granted him without more *advice*"; and comp. Shakespeare, *M. of V.* iv. 2. 6, "Bassanio upon more *advice*, Hath sent you here this ring"; also *Par. Lost*, ii. 376, "*Advise*, if this be worth Attempting," where 'advise' = consider. See also l. 755, note. *Scrupulous* = full of scruples, conscientious.
110. saws, sayings, maxims. *Saw*, *say*, and *saga* (a Norwegian legend) are cognate.
111. of purer fire, *i.e.* having a higher or diviner nature. (Or, as there is really no question of degree, we may render the phrase as = divine.) Compare the Platonic doctrine that each element had living creatures belonging to it, those of fire being the gods; similarly the Stoics held that whatever consisted of *pure fire* was divine, *e.g.* the stars: hence the additional significance of line 112.
112. the starry quire: an allusion to the music of the spheres; see lines 3, 1021. Pythagoras supposed that the planets emitted sounds proportional to their distances from the earth and formed a celestial concert too melodious to affect the "gross unpurgèd ear" of mankind: comp. l. 458 and *Arc.* 63-73. Shakespeare *(M. of V.* v. 1. 61) alludes to the music of the spheres:

> "There's not the smallest orb which thou behold'st
> But in his motion like an angel sings,
> Still quiring to the young-eyed cherubins," etc.

Quire is a form of *choir* (Lat. *chorus*, a band of singers); in Greek tragedy the chorus was supposed to represent the sentiments of the audience. *Quire* (of paper) is a totally different word, probably derived from Lat. *quatuor*, four.

113. nightly watchful spheres. Milton elsewhere alludes to the stars keeping watch: "And all the spangled host keep watch in order bright," *Hymn Nat.* 21. 'Nightly,' used as an adjective in the sense of 'nocturnal': comp. *Il Pens.* 84, "To bless the doors

from *nightly* harm"; *Arc.* 48, "*nightly* ill"; and Wordsworth's line: "The *nightly* hunter lifting up his eyes." Its ordinary sense is "night by night."

114. Lead in swift round. Comp. *Arc.* 71: "And the low world in measured motion draw, After the heavenly tune."

115. sounds, straits: A.S. *sund*, a strait of the sea, so called because it could be *swum* across. See Skeat, *Etym. Dict. s.v.*

116. to the moon, *i.e.* as affected by the moon. For similar uses of 'to,' comp. *Lyc.* 33, "tempered *to* the oaten flute"; *Lyc.* 44, "fanning their joyous leaves *to* thy soft lays." morrice. The waters quiver in the moonlight as if dancing. The morrice = a morris or Moorish dance, brought into Spain by the Moors, and thence introduced into England by John of Gaunt. We read also of a "morris-pike"—a weapon used by the Moors in Spain.

117. shelves, flat ledges of rock.

118. pert, lively. Here used in its radical sense (being a form of *perk*, smart): its modern sense is 'forward' or 'impertinent.' Skeat points out that *perk* and *pert* were both used as verbs; *e.g.* "*perked* up in a glistering grief," *Henry VIII.* ii. 3. 21: "how it (a child) speaks, and looks, and *perts* up the head," Beaumont and Fletcher's *Knight of the Burning Pestle*, i. 1. A similar change of *k* into *t* is seen in E. *mate* from M.E. *make*. dapper, quick (Du. *dapper*, Ger. *tapfer*, brave, quick). It is usual in the sense of 'neat.'

119. dimple. *Dimple* is a diminutive of *dip*, and cognate with *dingle* and *dapple*.

120. daisies trim: comp. *L'Alleg.* 75, "Meadows *trim*, with daisies pied"; *Il Pens.* 50, "*trim* gardens."

121. wakes, night-watches (A.S. *niht-wacu*, a night wake). The adjective *wakeful* (A.S. *wacol*) is the exact cognate of the Latin *vigil*. The word was applied to the vigil kept at the dedication of a church, then to the feast connected therewith, and finally to an evening merry-making. prove, test, judge of (Lat. *probare*). This is its sense in older writers and in the much-misunderstood phrase—"the exception *proves* the rule," which means that the exception is a test of the rule.

124. Venus now wakes, etc. Spenser, *Brit. Ida*, ii. 3, has "Night is Love's holyday." In this line wakens is used transitively, its object being 'Love.'
125. rights. Here used, as sometimes by Spenser, where modern usage requires *rites* (Lat. *ritus*, a custom): see l. 535.
126. daylight . . . sin. Daylight makes sin by revealing it. Contrast the sentiment of Comus with that of Milton in *Par. Lost*, i. 500, "When night Darkens the streets, then wander forth the sons Of Belial."
127. dun shades: evidently suggested by Fairfax's *Tasso*, ix. 62, "The horrid darkness, and the shadows *dun*." 'Dun' is A.S. *dunn*, dark.
129. Cotytto, the goddess of Licentiousness: here called 'dark-veiled' because her midnight orgies were veiled in darkness. She was a Thracian divinity, and her worshippers were called Baptae ('sprinkled'), because the ceremony of initiation involved the sprinkling of warm water.
131. called, invoked. dragon-womb Of Stygian darkness. The Styx (= 'the abhorred') was the chief river in the lower world. Milton here speaks of darkness as something positive, ejected from the womb of Night, Night being represented as a monster of the lower regions: comp. *Par. Lost*, i. 63. The pronoun 'her' shows that 'womb' is here used in its strict sense, but in *Par. Lost*, i. 673, "in his *womb* was hid metallic ore," it has the more general sense of "interior": comp. the use of Lat. *uterus*, *Aen.* ii. 258, vii. 499. dragon: Shakespeare refers to the dragons or 'dragon car' of night, *Cym.* ii. 2. 48, "Swift, swift, you *dragons* of the night"; *Tro. and Cress.* v. 8. 17, "The *dragon* wing of night o'erspreads the earth"; see also *Il Pens.* 59, "Cynthia checks her dragon yoke."
132. spets, a form of *spits* (as *spettle* for *spittle*).
133. one blot, *i.e.* a universal blot: comp. *Macbeth*, ii. 2. 63. Milton first wrote, "And makes a blot of nature."
134. Stay, here used causally = check. The radical sense of the word is 'to support,' as in the substantive *stay* and its plural *stays*. ebon, black as ebony. Ebony is so called because it is hard as a stone (Heb. *eben*, a stone); and the wood being of a dark colour, the name has become a synonym both for hardness and for blackness.

135. Hecat', *i.e.* Hecatè (as in line 535): a mysterious Thracian divinity, afterwards regarded as the goddess of witchcraft: for these reasons a fit companion for Cotytto and a fit patroness of Comus. Jonson calls her "the mistress of witches." She was supposed to send forth at night all kinds of demons and phantoms, and to wander about with the souls of the dead and amidst the howling of dogs.

136. utmost end, full completion. Compare *L'Alleg.* 109, "the corn That ten day-labourers could not *end*," where 'end' = 'complete.'

137. dues: see note, l. 12.

138. blabbing eastern scout, *i.e.* the tale-telling spy that comes from the East, viz. Morning.

139. nice; hard to please, fastidious: "a finely chosen epithet, expressing at once *curious* and *squeamish*" (Hurd). It is used by Comus in contempt: comp. ii. *Henry IV.* iv. 1, "Hence, therefore, thou *nice* crutch"; and see the index to the Globe *Shakespeare*. the Indian steep. In his *Elegia Tertia* Milton represents the sun as the "light-bringing king" whose home is on the shores of the Ganges *(i.e.* in the far East): comp. "the Indian mount," *Par. Lost*, i. 781, and Tennyson's *In Memoriam*, xxvi., "ere yet the morn Breaks hither over *Indian* seas."

140. cabined loop-hole: an allusion to the first glimpse of dawn, *i.e.* the peep of day. Comp. "Out of her window close she blushing peeps," said of the morning (P. Fletcher's *Eclogues*), as if the first rays of the sun struggled through some small aperture. 'Cabined,' literally 'belonging to a cabin,' and therefore small.

141. tell-tale Sun. Compare Spenser, *Brit. Ida*, ii. 3,

> "The thick-locked boughs shut out the *tell-tale* sun,
> For Venus hated his *all-blabbing* light."

Shakespeare refers to "the tell-tale day" *(R. of L.* 806). In *Odyssey*, viii., we read how Helios (the sun) kept watch and informed Vulcan of Venus's love for Mars. descry, etc., *i.e.* make known our hidden rites. 'Descry' is here used in its primary sense = *describe*: both words are from Lat. *describere*, to write fully. In Milton and Shakespeare 'descry' also occurs in the sense of 'to reconnoitre.'

142. solemnity, ceremony, rite. The word is from Lat. *sollus*, complete, and *annus*, a year; 'solemn' = *solennis* = *sollennis*. Hence the changes of meaning: (1) recurring at the end of a completed year; (2) usual; (3) religious, for sacred festivals recur at stated intervals; (4) that which is not to be lightly undertaken, *i.e.* serious or important.

143. knit hands, etc. Comp. *Masque of Hymen*:

> "Now, now begin to set
> Your spirits in active heat;
> And, since your hands are met,
> Instruct your nimble feet,
> In motions swift and meet,
> The happy ground to beat."

144. light fantastic round: comp. *L'Alleg.* 34, "Come, and trip it, as you go, On the light fantastic toe." A round is a dance or 'measure' in which the dancers join hands, 'Fantastic' = full of fancy, unrestrained. So Shakespeare uses it of that which has merely been imagined, and has not yet happened. It is now used in the sense of grotesque. *Fancy* is a form of *fantasy* (Greek *phantasia*).

At this point in the mask Comus and his rout dance a measure, after which he again speaks, but in a different strain. The change is marked by a return to blank verse: the previous lines are mostly in octosyllabic couplets.

145. different, *i.e.* different from the voluptuous footing of Comus and his crew.

146. footing: comp. *Lyc.* 103, "Camus, reverend sire, went *footing* slow."

147. shrouds, coverts, places of hiding. The word etymologically denotes 'something cut off,' being allied to 'shred'; hence a garment; and finally (as in Milton) any covering or means of covering. Many of Latimer's sermons are described as having been "preached in The Shrouds," a covered place near St. Paul's Cathedral. The modern use of the word is restricted: comp. l. 316. brakes, bushes. Shakespeare has "hawthorn-*brake*," *M. N. D.* iii. l. 3, and the word seems to be connected with *bracken*.

148. Some virgin sure, *sc.* 'it is.'

150. charms ... wily trains; *i.e.* spells ... cunning allurements. *Charm* is the Lat. *carmen*, a song, also used in the sense of 'magic verses'; wily = full of *wile* (etymologically the same as guile). *Train* here denotes an artifice or snare as in 'venereal trains' *(Sams. Agon.* 533): "Oh, *train* me not, sweet mermaid, with thy note" *(Com. of Errors*, iii. 2. 45). See Index, Globe *Shakespeare.* Some would take 'wily trains' as = trains of wiles.

151. ere long: *ere* has here the force of a preposition; in A.S. it was an adverb as well = soon, but now it is used only as a conjunction or a preposition.

153. Thus I hurl, etc. "Conceive that at this moment of the performance the actor who personates Comus flings into the air, or makes a gesture as if flinging into the air, some powder, which, by a stage-device, is kindled so as to produce a flash of blue light. In the original draft among the Cambridge MSS. the phrase is *powdered spells*; but Milton, by a judicious change, concealing the mechanism of the stage-trick, substituted *dazzling*" (Masson).

154. dazzling. This implies both brightness and illusion. spells. A *spell* is properly a magical form of words (A.S. *spel*, a saying): here it refers to the whole enchantment employed. spongy air: so called because it holds in suspension the magic powder.

155. Of power to cheat ... and (to) give, etc. These lines are attributive to 'spells.' The preposition 'of' is thus used to denote a characteristic; thus 'of power' = powerful; comp. l. 677. blear illusion; deception, that which deceives by *blurring* the vision. Shakespeare has 'bleared thine eye' = dimmed thy vision, deceived *(Tam. Shrew*, v. 1. 120). Comp. "This may stand for a pretty superficial argument, to *blear* our eyes, and lull us asleep in security" (Sir W. Raleigh). *Blur* is another form of *blear.*

156. presentments, appearances. This word is to be distinguished from *presentiment.* A presentiment is a "fore-feeling" (Lat. *praesentire*): while a presentment is something presented (Lat. *praesens*, being before). Shakespeare, *Ham.* iii. 4. 54, has 'presentment' in the sense of picture. quaint habits, unfamiliar dress. Quaint is from Lat. *cognitus*, so that its primary sense is 'known' or 'remarkable.' In French it became *coint*, which was treated as if from Lat. *comptus*, neat; hence the word is frequent

in the sense of neat, exact, or delicate. Its modern sense is 'unusual' or 'odd.'

158. suspicious flight: flight due to suspicion of danger.

160. I, under fair pretence, etc.: 'Under the mask of friendly intentions and with the plausible language of wheedling courtesy, I insinuate myself into the unsuspecting mind and ensnare it.'

161. glozing, flattering, wheedling. Compare *Par. Lost*, ix. 549,

> "So *glozed* the temper, and his proem tuned:
> Into the heart of Eve his words made way."

Gloze is from the old word *glose*, a gloss or explanation (Gr. *glossa*, the tongue): hence also glossary, glossology, etc. Trench, in his lecture on the Morality of Words, points out how often fair names are given to ugly things: it is in this way that a word which merely denoted an explanation has come to denote a false explanation, an endeavour to deceive. The word has no connection with *gloss* = brightness.

162. Baited, rendered attractive. Radically *bait* is the causative of *bite*; hence a trap is said to be baited. Comp. *Sams. Ag.* 1066, "The *bait* of honied words."

163. wind me, etc. The verbs *wind (i.e.* coil) and *hug* suggest the cunning of the serpent. The easy-hearted man is the person whose heart or mind is easily overcome: 'man' is here used generically. Burton, in *Anat. of Mel.*, says: "The devil, being a slender incomprehensible spirit, can easily insinuate and *wind* himself into human bodies." *Me* is here used reflexively: see note, l. 61. This is not the ethic dative.

165. virtue, *i.e.* power or influence (Lat. *virtus*). This radical sense is still found in the phrase 'by virtue of' = by the power of. The adjective *virtuous* is now used only of moral excellence: in line 621 it has its older meaning.

166. The reading of the text is that of the editions of 1637 and 1645. In the edition of 1673 the reading was:
> "I shall appear some harmless villager,
> And hearken, if I may, her business here.
> But here she comes, I fairly step aside."

But in the errata there was a direction to omit the comma after *may*, and to change *here* into *hear*. In Masson's text, accordingly, he reads: "And hearken, if I may her business hear."

167. keeps up, etc., *i.e.* keeps occupied with his country affairs even up to a late hour. *Gear*: its original sense is 'preparation' (A.S. *gearu*, ready); hence 'business' or 'property.' Comp. Spenser, F. Q. vi. 3. 6, "That to Sir Calidore was *easy gear*," *i.e.* an easy matter, fairly, softly. *Fair* and *softly* were two words which went together, signifying *gently* (Warton).

170. mine ear ... My best guide. Observe the juxtaposition of *mine* and *my* in these lines. *Mine* is frequent before a vowel, especially when the possessive adjective is not emphatic. In Shakespeare 'mine' is almost always found before "eye," "ear," etc., where no emphasis is intended (Abbott, § 237).

171. Methought, *i.e.* it seemed to me. In the verb 'methinks' *me* is the dative, and *thinks* is an impersonal verb (A.S. *thincan*, to appear), quite distinct from the causal verb 'I think,' which is from A.S. *thencan*, to make to appear.

173. jocund, merry. Comp. *L'Allegro*, 94, "the *jocund* rebecks sound." gamesome, lively. This word, like many other adjectives in -*some*, is now less common than it was in Elizabethan English: many such adjectives are obsolete, *e.g.* laboursome, joysome, quietsome, etc. (see Trench's *English, Past and Present*, v.).

174. unlettered hinds, ignorant rustics (A.S. *hina*, a domestic).

175. granges, granaries, barns (Lat. *granum*, grain). The word is now applied to a farm-house with its outhouses.

176. Pan, the god of everything connected with pastoral life: see *Arc.* 106, "Though Syrinx your Pan's mistress were."

177. thank the gods amiss. *Amiss* stands for M.E. *on misse* = in error. "Perhaps there is a touch of Puritan rigour in this. The gods should be thanked in solemn acts of devotion, and not by merry-making" (Keightley). See Introduction.

178. swilled insolence, etc., *i.e.* the drunken rudeness of those carousing at this late hour. *Swill*: to swill is to drink greedily, hence to drink like a pig. wassailers; from 'wassail' [A.S. *waes hael*; from *wes*, be thou, and *hál*, whole (modern English *hale*)], a form of salutation, used in drinking one's health; and hence employed in the sense of 'revelling' or 'carousing.' The

'wassail-bowl' here referred to is the "spicy nutbrown ale" of *L'Allegro*, 100. In Scott's *Ivanhoe*, the Friar drinks to the Black Knight with the words, *"Waes hale*, Sir Sluggish Knight," the Knight replying "Drink *hale*, Holy Clerk."

180. inform . . . feet. Comp. *Sams. Agon.* 335: "hither hath *informed* your younger *feet*." This use of 'inform' (= direct) is well illustrated in Spenser's *F. Q.* vi. 6: "Which with sage counsel, when they went astray, He could *enforme*, and then reduce aright."

184. spreading favour. Epithet transferred from cause to effect.

187. kind hospitable woods: an instance of the pathetic fallacy which attributes to inanimate objects the feelings of men: comp. ll. 194, 195. *As* in this line (after *such*) has the force of a relative pronoun.

188. grey-hooded Even. Comp. "sandals grey," *Lyc.* 187; "civil-suited," *Il Pens.* 122; both applied to morning.

189. a sad votarist, etc. A votarist is one who is bound by a vow (Lat. *votum*): the current form is *votary*, applied in a general sense to one *devoted* to an object, *e.g.* a votary of science. In the present case, the votarist is a *palmer*, *i.e.* a pilgrim who carried a palm-branch in token of his having been to Palestine. Such would naturally wear sober-coloured or homely garments: comp. Drayton, "a palmer poor in homely russet clad." In *Par. Reg.* xiv. 426, Morning is a pilgrim clad in "amice grey." On weed, see note, l. 16.

190. hindmost wheels: comp. l. 95: "If this fine image is optically realised, what we see is Evening succeeding Day as the figure of a venerable grey-hooded mendicant might slowly follow the wheels of some rich man's chariot" (Masson).

192. labour . . . thoughts, the burden of my thoughts.

193. engaged, committed: this use of the word may be compared with that in *Hamlet*, iii. 3. 69, "Art more *engaged*" (= bound or entangled). To *engage* is to bind by a *gage* or pledge.

195. stole, stolen. This use of the past form for the participle is frequent in Elizabethan English. Else, etc. The meaning is: 'The envious darkness must have stolen my brothers, *otherwise* why should night hide the light of the stars?' The clause 'but for some felonious end' is therefore to some extent tautological.

197. **dark lantern.** The stars by a far-fetched metaphor are said to be concealed, though not extinguished, just as the light of a dark lantern is shut off by a slide. Comp. More; "Vice is like a *dark lanthorn*, which turns its bright side only to him that bears it."

198. **everlasting oil.** Comp. *F. Q.* i. 1. 57:
"By this the eternal lamps, wherewith high Jove
Doth light the lower world, were half yspent:"
also *Macbeth*, ii. 1. 5, "There's husbandry in heaven; Their candles are all out." There is here an irregularity of syntax. "That Nature hung in heaven" is a relative clause co-ordinate *in sense* with the next clause; but by a change of thought the phrase "and filled their lamps" is treated as a principal clause, and a new object is introduced: comp. l. 6.

203. **rife**, prevalent. **perfect**, distinct; see note, l. 73.

204. **single darkness**, darkness only. *Single* is from the same base as *simple*; comp. l. 369.

205. **What might this be?** This is a direct question about a past event, and has the same meaning as "what should it be?" in line 482: see note there. **A thousand fantasies**, etc. On this passage Lowell says: "That wonderful passage in *Comus* of the airy tongues, perhaps the most imaginative in suggestion he ever wrote, was conjured out of a dry sentence in Purchas's abstract of Marco Polo. Such examples help us to understand the poet." Reference may also be made to the *Anat. of Mel.*: "Fear makes our imagination conceive what it list, ... and tyrannizeth over our fantasy more than all other affections, especially in the dark"; also to the song prefixed to the same work, "My phantasie presents a thousand ugly shapes," etc. On the power of imagination or phantasy, Shakespeare says:

"As imagination bodies forth
The forms of things unknown, the poet's pen
Turns them to *shapes*, and gives to *airy nothing*
A local habitation and a name."—

M. N. D. v. 1. 14.

Compare also Ben Jonson's *Vision of Delight*:
"Break, Phant'sie, from thy cave of cloud,
And spread thy purple wings;
Now all thy figures are allow'd,

>   And various shapes of things:
>   Create of *airy forms* a stream . . .
>   And though it be a waking dream," etc.

207. Of calling shapes, etc. In Heywood's *Hierarchy of Angels* there is a reference to travellers seeing strange shapes beckoning to them. Such words as 'shapes,' 'shadows,' 'airy tongues,' etc., illustrate Milton's power to create an indefinite, yet expressive picture. Comp. *Aen.* iv. 460. beckoning shadows dire. A characteristic arrangement of words in Milton: comp. lines 470, 945.

208. syllable, pronounce distinctly.

210. may startle well, may well startle.

212. siding champion, Conscience. To side is to take a side, and hence to assist: comp. *Cor.* iv. 2. 2: "The nobles who have *sided* in his behalf." 'Conscience' (here a trisyllable) is used in its current sense: in *Son.* xxii. 10 it means consciousness. Comp. *Hen. VIII.* iii. 2. 379: "A peace above all earthly dignities, A still and quiet Conscience."

213. pure-eyed Faith. Comp. *Lyc.* 81, "those pure eyes And perfect witness of all-judging Jove"; also the Scriptural words, "God is of purer eyes than to behold iniquity." The maiden, whose safeguard is her purity, calls on Faith, Hope, and Chastity, each being characterised by an epithet denoting purity of thought and act, viz. 'pure-eyed,' 'white-handed,' and 'unblemished.' The placing of Chastity instead of Charity in the trio is significant: see i. *Cor.* xiii.

214. hovering angel. Hope hovers over the maiden to protect her. The word 'hover' is found frequently in the sense of 'shelter.' girt, surrounded. golden wings. In *Il Pens.* 52, Contemplation "soars on golden wing."

216. see ye visibly, *i.e.* you are not mere shapes, but living presences. *Ye*: here the object of the verb. "This confusion between *ye* and *you* did not exist in old English; *ye* was always used as a nominative, and *you* as a dative or accusative. In the English Bible the distinction is very carefully observed, but in the dramatists of the Elizabethan period there is a very loose use of the two forms" (Morris). It is so in Milton, who has *ye* as nominative, accusative, and dative; comp. lines 513, 967, 1020; also *Arc.* 40, 81, 101. It may be noted that *ye* can be

pronounced more rapidly than *you*, and is therefore frequent when an unaccented syllable is required.

217. the Supreme Good. God being the Supreme Good, if evil exists, it must exist for God's purposes. Evil exists for the sake of 'vengeance' or punishment.

219. glistering guardian, *i.e.* one clad in the 'pure ambrosial weeds' of l. 16. *Glister, glisten, glitter,* and *glint* are cognate words.

221. Was I deceived? There is a break in the construction at the end of line 220. The girl's trust in Heaven is suddenly strengthened by a glimpse of light in the dark sky. Warton regards the repetition of the same words in lines 223, 224 as beautifully expressing the confidence of an unaccusing conscience.

222. her = its. In Latin *nubes*, a cloud, is feminine.

223. does ... turn ... and casts. Comp. *Il Pens.* 46, 'doth diet' and 'hears.' When two co-ordinate verbs are of the same tense and mood the auxiliary verb should apply to both. The above construction is due probably to change of thought.

225. tufted grove. Comp. *L'Alleg.* 78: "bosomed high in *tufted trees.*"

226. hallo. Also *hallow* (as in Milton's editions), *halloo, halloa,* and *holloa.*

227. make to be heard. Make = cause.

228. new-enlivened spirits, *i.e.* my spirits that have been newly enlivened: for the form of the compound adjective comp. note, l. 36.

229. they, *i.e.* the brothers.

230. Echo. In classical mythology she was a nymph whom Juno punished by preventing her from speaking before others or from being silent after others had spoken. She fell in love with Narcissus, and pined away until nothing remained of her but her voice. Compare the invocation to Echo in Ben Jonson's *Cynthia's Revels,* i. 1.

The lady's song, which has been described as "an address to the very Genius of Sound," is here very naturally introduced. The lady wishes to rouse the echoes of the wood in order to attract her brothers' notice, and she does so by addressing Echo, who grieves for the lost youth Narcissus as the lady grieves for her lost brothers.

231. thy airy shell; the atmosphere. Comp. "the hollow round of Cynthia's seat," *Hymn Nat.* 103. The marginal reading in the MS. is *cell*. Some suppose that 'shell' is here used, like Lat. *concha*, because in classical times various musical instruments were made in the form of a shell.

232. Meander's margent green. Maeander, a river of Asia Minor, remarkable for the windings of its course; hence the verb 'to meander,' and hence also (in Keightley's opinion) the mention of the river as a haunt of Echo. It is more probable, however, that, as the lady addresses Echo as the "Sweet Queen of Parley" and the unhappy lover of the lost Narcissus, the river is here mentioned because of its associations with music and misfortune. The Marsyas was a tributary of the Maeander, and the legend was that the flute upon which Marsyas played in his rash contest with Apollo was carried into the Maeander and, after being thrown on land, dedicated to Apollo, the god of song. Comp. *Lyc.* 58-63, where the Muses and misfortune are similarly associated by a reference to Orpheus, whose 'gory visage' and lyre were carried "down the swift Hebrus to the Lesbian shore." Further, the Maeander is associated with the sorrows of the maiden Byblis, who seeks her lost brother Caunus (called by Ovid *Maeandrius juvenis*). [Since the above was written, Prof. J. W. Hales has given the following explanation of Milton's allusion: "The real reason is that the Meander was a famous haunt of swans, and the swan was a favourite bird with the Greek and Latin writers—one to whose sweet singing they perpetually allude" *(Athenaeum*, April 20, 1889).] 'Margent.' *Marge* and *margin* are forms of the same word.

233. the violet-embroidered vale. The notion that flowers *broider* or ornament the ground is common in poetry: comp. *Par. Lost*, iv. 700: "Under foot the violet, Crocus, and hyacinth, with rich inlay *Broidered* the ground." In *Lyc.* 148, the flowers themselves wear 'embroidery.' The nightingale is made to haunt a violet-embroidered vale because these flowers are associated with love (see Jonson's *Masque of Hymen*) and with innocence (see *Hamlet*, iv. 5. 158: "I would give you some violets, but they withered all when my father died"). Prof. Hales, however, thinks that some particular vale is here alluded to, and argues, with much acumen, that the poet referred to the woodlands close

83

by Athens to the north-west, through which the Cephissus flowed, and where stood the birthplace of Sophocles, who sings of his native Colonus as frequented by nightingales. The same critic regards the epithet 'violet-embroidered' as a translation of the Greek ἰοστέφανος (= crowned with violets), frequently applied by Aristophanes to Athens, of which Colonus was a suburb. Macaulay also refers to Athens as "the violet-crowned city." It is, at least, very probable that Milton might here associate the nightingale with Colonus, as he does in *Par. Reg.* iv. 245: see the following note.

234. love-lorn nightingale, the nightingale whose loved ones are lost: comp. Virgil, *Georg.* iv. 511: "As the nightingale wailing in the poplar shade plains for her lost young, . . . while she weeps the night through, and sitting on a bough, reproduces her piteous melody, and fills the country round with the plaints of her sorrow." *Lorn* and *lost* are cognate words, the former being common in the compound *forlorn*: see note, l. 39. Milton makes frequent allusion to the nightingale: in *Il Penseroso* it is 'Philomel'; in *Par. Reg.* iv. 245, it is 'the Attic bird'; and in *Par. Lost* viii. 518, it is 'the amorous bird of night.' He calls it the Attic bird in allusion to the story of Philomela, the daughter of Pandion, King of Athens. Near the Academy was Colonus, which Sophocles has celebrated as the haunt of nightingales (Browne). Philomela was changed, at her own prayer, into a nightingale that she might escape the vengeance of her brother-in-law Tereus. The epithet 'love-lorn,' however, seems to point to the legend of A{=e}don (Greek +aêdôn+, a nightingale), who, having killed her own son by mistake, was changed into a nightingale, whose mournful song was represented by the Greek poets as the lament of the mother for her child.

235. her sad song mourneth, *i.e.* sings her plaintive melody. 'Sad song' forms a kind of cognate accusative.

237. likest thy Narcissus. Narcissus, who failed to return the love of Echo, was punished by being made to fall in love with his own image reflected in a fountain: this he could never approach, and he accordingly pined away and was changed into the flower which bears his name. See the dialogue between Mercury and Echo in *Cynthia's Revels*, i. 1. Grammatically, *likest*

is an adjective qualified adverbially by "(to) thy Narcissus": comp. *Il Pens.* 9, "likest hovering dreams."

238. have hid. This is not a grammatical inaccuracy (as Warton thinks), but the subjunctive mood.

240. Tell me but where, *i.e.* 'Only tell me where.'

241. Sweet Queen of Parley, etc. 'Parley is conversation (Fr. *parler*, to speak): *parlour*, *parole*, *palaver*, *parliament*, *parlance*. etc., are cognate. Daughter of the Sphere, *i.e.* of the sphere which is her "airy shell" (l. 231): comp. "Sphere-born harmonious sisters, Voice and Verse" *(At a Solemn Music*, 2).

243. give resounding grace, etc., *i.e.* add the charm of echo to the music of the spheres.

The metrical structure of this song should be noted: the lines vary in length from two to six feet. The rhymes are few, and the effect is more striking owing to the consonance of *shell*, *well* with *vale*, *nightingale*; also of *pair*, *where* with *are* and *sphere*; and of *have* with *cave*. Masson regards this song as a striking illustration of Milton's free use of imperfect rhymes, even in his most musical passages.

244. mortal mixture ... divine enchanting ravishment. The words *mortal* and *divine* are in antithesis: comp. *Il Pens.* 91, 92, "The immortal mind that hath forsook Her mansion in this fleshly nook." The lines embody a compliment to the Lady Alice: read in this connection lines 555 and 564. 'Ravishment,' rapture (a cognate word) or ecstasy: comp. *Il Pens.* 40, "Thy rapt soul sitting in thine eyes"; also l. 794.

246. Sure, used adverbially: comp. line 493, and 'certain,' l. 266.

247. vocal, used proleptically.

248. his = its: see note, l. 96. The pronoun refers to 'something holy.'

251. smoothing the raven down. As the nightingale's song smooths the rugged brow of Night *(Il Pens.* 58), so here the song of the lady smooths the raven plumage of darkness. In classical mythology Night is a winged goddess.

252. it, *i.e.* darkness.

253. Circe ... Sirens three. In the *Odyssey* the Sirens are two in number and have no connection with Circe. They lived on a rocky island off the coast of Sicily and near the rock of Scylla (l. 257), and lured sailors to destruction by the charm

of their song. Circe was also a sweet singer and had the power of enchanting men; hence the combined allusion: see also Horace's *Epist.* i. 2, 23, *Sirenum voces, et Circes pocula nôsti.* Besides, the Sirens were daughters of the river-god Achelous, and Circe had Naiads or fountain-nymphs among her maids.

254. flowery-kirtled Naiades: fresh-water nymphs dressed in flowers, or having their skirts decorated with flowers. A *kirtle* is a gown; Skeat suggests that it is a diminutive of *skirt.*

255. baleful, injurious (A.S. *balu*, evil).

256. sung. "The verbs *swim, begin, run, drink, shrink, sink, ring, sing, spring*, have for their proper past tenses *swam, began, ran*, etc., preserving the original *a*; but in older writers (sixteenth and seventeenth centuries) and in colloquial English we find forms with *u*, which have come from the passive participles." (Morris). take the prisoned soul, *i.e.* would take the soul prisoner; 'prisoned' being used proleptically.

257. lap it in Elysium. *Lap* is a form of wrap: comp. *L'Alleg.* 136, "*Lap* me in soft Lydian airs." Elysium: the abode of the spirits of the blessed; comp. *L'Alleg.* 147, "heaped Elysian flowers." Scylla ... Charybdis. The former, a rival of Circe in the affections of the sea-god Glaucus, was changed into a monster, surrounded by barking dogs. She threw herself into the sea and became a rock, the noise of the surrounding waves ("multis circum latrantibus undis," *Aen.* vii. 588) resembling the barking of dogs. The latter was a daughter of Poseidon, and was hurled by Zeus into the sea, where she became a whirlpool.

260. slumber: comp. *Pericles*, v. 1. 335, "thick slumber Hangs upon mine eyes."

261. madness, ecstasy. The same idea is expressed in *Il Pens.* 164: "As may with sweetness, through mine ear, Dissolve me into *ecstasies*, And bring all heaven before mine eyes." In Shakespeare 'ecstasy' occurs in the sense of madness; see *Hamlet*, iii. 1. 167, "That unmatched form and feature of blown youth, Blasted with *ecstasy*"; *Temp.* iii. 3. 108, "hinder them from what this *ecstasy* May now provoke them to": comp. also "the pleasure of that madness," *Wint. Tale*, v. 3. 73. See also l. 625.

262. home-felt, deeply felt. Compare "The *home* thrust of a friendly sword is sure" (Dryden); "This is a consideration that comes

home to our interest" (Addison): see also Index to Globe *Shakespeare*.

263. waking bliss, as opposed to the ecstatic slumber induced by the song of Circe.

265. Hail, foreign wonder! Warton notes that *Comus* is universally allowed to have taken some of its tints from the *Tempest*, and quotes, "O you wonder! If you be maid, or no?" i. 2. 426.

266. certain: see note, l. 246.

267. Unless the goddess, etc. = unless *thou be* the goddess that in rural shrine *dwells* here. Here, as often in Latin, we have 'unless' (Lat. *nisi*, etc.) used with a single word instead of a clause: and, also as in Latin, the verb in the relative clause has the person of the antecedent.

268. Pan or Sylvan: see l. 176: also *Il Pens.* 134, "shadows brown that Sylvan loves," and *Arc.* 106, "Though Syrinx your Pan's mistress were." Sylvanus, the god of fields and forests, as denoted by his name which is corrupted from Silvan (Lat. *silva*, a wood).

269. Forbidding, etc. These lines recall the language of *Arcades*, in which also a lady is complimented as "a *deity*," "a *rural* Queen," and "mistress of yon princely shrine" in the land of Pan. There is a reference also to her protecting the woods through her servant, the Genius: *Arc.* 36-53, 91-95.

271. ill is lost. A Latin idiom (as Keightley points out) = *male perditur*. Prof. Masson, however, would regard it as equivalent to "there is little loss in losing."

273. extreme shift; last resource. Comp. l. 617.

274. my severed company: a condensed expression = the companions separated from me. Comp. l. 315: this figure of speech is called Synecdoche.

277. What chance, etc. In lines 277-290 we have a reproduction of that form of dialogue employed in Greek tragedy in which question and answer occupy alternate lines: it is called *stichomythia*, and is admirable when there is a gradual rise in excitement towards the end (as in the *Supplices* of Euripides). In *Samson Agonistes*, which is modelled on the Greek pattern, Milton did not employ it.

278. An alliterative line.

279. near ushering, closely attending. To usher is to introduce (Lat. *ostium*, a door).

284. twain: thus frequently used as a predicate. It is also used after its substantive as in *Lyc.* 110, "of metals *twain*," and as a substantive.

285. forestalling, anticipating. 'Forestall,' originally a marketing term, is to buy up goods before they have been displayed at a *stall* in the market in order to sell them again at a higher price: hence 'to anticipate.' prevented. 'Prevent,' now used in the sense of 'hinder,' seems in this line to have something of its older meaning, viz., to anticipate (in which case 'forestalling' would be proleptic). Comp. l. 362; *Par. Lost*, vi. 129, "half-way he met His daring foe, at this *prevention* more Incensed."

286. to hit. This is the gerundial infinitive after an adjective: comp. "good to eat," "deadly to hear," etc.

287. Imports their loss, etc.: 'Apart from the present emergency, is the loss of them important?'

289. manly prime, etc.: 'Were they in the prime of manhood, or were they merely youths?' With Milton the 'prime of manhood' is where 'youth' ends: comp. *Par. Lost*, xi. 245, *"prime* in manhood where youth ended"; iii. 636, "a stripling Cherub he appears, Not of the prime, yet such as in his face Youth smiled celestial." Spenser has 'prime' = Spring.

290. Hebe, the goddess of youth. "The down of manhood" had not appeared on the lips of the brothers.

291. what time: common in poetry for 'when' (Lat. *quo tempore*). Compare Horace, *Od.* iii. 6: "what time the sun shifted the shadows of the mountains, and took the yokes from the wearied oxen." laboured: wearied with labour.

292. loose traces. Because no longer taut from the draught of the plough.

293. swinked, overcome with toil, fatigued (A.S. *swincan*, to toil). Skeat points out that this was once an extremely common word; the sense of toil is due to that of constant movement from the *swinging* of the labourer's arms. In Chaucer 'swinker' = ploughman.

294. mantling, spreading. To mantle is strictly to cloak or cover: comp. *Temp.* v. 1. 67, "fumes that *mantle* Their clearer reason."

297. port, bearing, mien.

298. faery. This spelling is nearer to that of the M.E. *faerie* than the current form.
299. the element; the air. Since the time of the Greek philosopher Empedocles, fire, earth, air, and water have been popularly called the four elements; when used alone, however, 'the element' commonly means 'the air.' Comp. *Hen. V.* iv. 1. 107, "The *element* shows him as it doth to me"; *Par. Lost*, ii. 490, "the louring *element* Scowls o'er the darkened landscape snow or shower," etc.
301. plighted, interwoven or *plaited*. The verb 'plight' (or more properly *plite*) is a variant of *plait*: see *Il Pens.* 57, "her sweetest saddest *plight*." The word has no connection with 'plight,' l. 372. awe-strook. Milton uses three forms of the participle, viz. 'strook,' 'struck,' and 'strucken.'
302. worshiped. The final consonant is now doubled in such verbs before *-ed*.
303. were = would be: subjunctive. like the path to Heaven; *i.e.* it would be a pleasure to help, etc. There is (probably) no allusion to the Scripture parable of the narrow and difficult way to Heaven *(Matt.* vii.) as in *Son.* ix., "labours up the hill of heavenly Truth."
304. help you find: comp. l. 623. The simple infinitive is here used without *to* where *to* would now be inserted. This omission of the preposition now occurs with so few verbs that 'to' is often called the sign of the infinitive, but in Early English the only sign of the infinitive was the termination *en (e.g.* he can *speken*). The infinitive, being used as a noun, had a dative form called the gerund, which was preceded by the preposition *to*, and when this became confused with the simple infinitive the use of *to* became general. Comp. *Son.* xx. 4, *"Help* waste a sullen day."
305. readiest way. Here 'readiest' logically belongs to the predicate.
311. each ... every: see note, l. 19. alley, a walk or avenue.
312. Dingle ... bushy dell ... bosky bourn. 'Dingle' = dimble (see Ben Jonson's *Sad Shepherd*) = dimple = a little dip or depression; hence a narrow valley. 'Dell' = dale, literally a cleft; hence a valley, not so deep as a dingle. 'Bosky bourn,' a stream whose banks are bushy or thickly grown with bushes. 'Bourn,'

a boundary, is a distinct word etymologically, but the phrase "from side to side," as used by Comus, might well imply that the valley as well as the stream is here referred to. 'Bosky,' bushy. The noun 'boscage' = jungle or *bush* (M.E. *busch, bush, bush*). 'See Tennyson's *Dream of F. W.* 243, "the sombre *boscage* of the wood."

315. stray attendance = strayed attendants; abstract for concrete, as in line 274. Comp. *Par. Lost*, x. 80, *"Attendance* none shall need, nor train"; xii. 132, "Of herds, and flocks, and numerous *servitude"* (= servants).

316. shroud, etc. Milton first wrote "within these shroudie limits": see note, l. 147.

317. low roosted lark, *i.e.* the lark that has roosted on the ground. This is certainly Milton's meaning, as he refers to the bird as rising from its "thatched pallet" = its nest, which is built on the ground. 'Roost' has, however, no radical connection with *rest*, but denotes a perch for fowls, and Keightley's remark that Milton is guilty of supposing the lark to sleep, like a hen, upon a perch or roost, may therefore be noticed. But the poets' meaning is obvious. Prof. Masson takes 'thatched' as referring to the texture of the nest or to the corn-stalks or rushes over it.

318. rouse. Here used intransitively = awake.

322. honest-offered: see notes, ll. 36, 228.

323. sooner, more readily.

324. tapestry halls. Halls hung with tapestry, tapestry being "a kind of carpet work, with wrought figures, especially used for decorating walls." The word is said to be from the Persian.

325. first was named. The meaning is: *'Courtesy* which is derived from *court*, and which is still nominally most common in high life, is nevertheless most readily found amongst those of humble station.' This sentiment is becoming in the mouth of Lady Alice when addressed to a humble shepherd. 'Courtesy' (or, as Milton elsewhere writes, *courtship*) has, like *civility*, lost much of its deeper significance. Comp. Spenser, *F. Q.* vi. 1. 1:

> "Of Court it seems men Courtesy do call,
> For that it there most useth to abound."

327. less warranted, *i.e.* when I have less *guarantee* of safety. *Guarantee* and *warrant*, like *guard* and *ward*, *guile* and *wile*, are radically the same.

329. Eye me, *i.e.* look on me. To *eye* a person now usually implies watching narrowly or suspiciously. square, accommodate, adjust. The adj. 'proportioned' is here used proleptically, denoting the result of the action indicated by the verb 'square.' Comp. *M. for M.* v. 1: "Thou 'rt said to have a stubborn soul, ... And *squar'st* thy life accordingly." Exeunt, *i.e.* they go out, they leave the stage.

331. Unmuffle, uncover yourselves. To *muffle* is to cover up, *e.g.* 'to *muffle* the throat,' 'a *muffled* sound,' etc. *Muffle* (subst.) is a diminutive of *muff*.

332. wont'st, *i.e.* art wont. *Wont'st* is here apparently the 2nd person singular, present tense, of a verb *to wont* = to be accustomed; hence also the participle *wonted (Il Pens.* 37, "keep thy *wonted* state"). But the M.E. verb was *wonen*, to dwell or be accustomed, and its participle *woned* or *wont*. The fact that *wont* was a participle being forgotten, it was treated as a distinct verb, and a new participle formed, viz., *wonted* (= won-ed-ed); from this again comes the noun *wontedness*. Milton, however, uses *wont* as a present only twice in his poetry: as in modern English he uses it as a noun (= custom) or as a participial adj. with the verb *to be (Il Pens.* 123, "As she was wont"). benison, blessing: radically the same as 'benediction' (Lat. *benedictio*).

333. Stoop thy pale visage, etc. Comp. l. 1023 and *Il Pens.* 72, "*Stooping* through a fleecy cloud." 'Visage,' a word now mostly used with a touch of contempt, in Milton simply denotes 'face': see *Il Pens.* 13, "saintly *visage*"; *Lyc.* 62, "His gory *visage* down the stream was sent." amber: comp. *L'Alleg.* 61, "Robed in flames and *amber* light," and Tennyson:

"What time the *amber* morn

Forth gushes from beneath a low-hung cloud."

334. disinherit, drive out, dispossess. Comp. *Two Gent.* iii. 2. 87, "This or else nothing, will *inherit (i.e.* obtain possession of) her."

336. Influence ... dammed up. The verb here shows that influence is employed in its strict sense, = a flowing in (Lat. *in* and *fluo*): it was thus used in astrology to denote "an *influent* course of

91

the planets, their virtue being infused into, or their course working on, inferior creatures"; comp. *L'Alleg.* 112, "whose bright eyes Rain *influence*"; *Par. Lost*, iv. 669, "with kindly heat Of various *influence*." Astrology has left many traces upon the English language, *e.g.* influence, disastrous, ill-starred, ascendant, etc. See also l. 360.

337. taper; here a vocative, the verb being "visit (thou)."

338. though a rush candle, *i.e.* 'though it be only a rush-candle'; a rush light, obtained from the pith of a rush dipped in oil.

340. long levelled rule; straight horizontal beam of light: comp. *Par. Lost*, iv. 543, "the setting sun ... *Levelled* his evening rays." The instrument with which straight lines are drawn is called a *rule* or ruler.

341. star of Arcady Or Tyrian Cynosure; here put by synecdoche for 'lode-star.' More particularly, the star of Arcady signifies any of the stars in the constellation of the Great Bear, by which Greek sailors steered; and 'Tyrian Cynosure' signifies the stars comprising that part of the constellation of the Lesser Bear which, from its shape, was called *Cynosura*, the dog's tail (Greek +kynos oura+), and by which Phoenician or Tyrian sailors steered. See *L'Alleg.* 80, "The *cynosure* of neighbouring eyes," where the word is used as a common noun = point of attraction. Both constellations are connected in Greek mythology with the Arcadian nymph Callisto, who was turned by Zeus into the Great Bear while her son Arcas became the Lesser Bear. Milton follows the Roman poets in associating these stars with Arcadia on this account.

343. barred, debarred or barred *from*.

344. wattled cotes: enclosures made of hurdles, *i.e.* frames of plaited twigs. *Cote*, *cot*, and *coat* are varieties of the same word = a covering or enclosure.

345. oaten stops: see *Lyc.* 33, "the *oaten* flute"; 88, "But now my *oat* proceeds"; 188, "the tender stops of various *quills*." The shepherd's pipe, being at first a row of oaten stalks, "the oaten pipe," "oat," etc., came to denote any instrument of this kind and even to signify "pastoral poetry." The 'stops' are the holes over which the player's fingers are placed, also called vent-holes or "ventages" *(Ham.* iii. 2. 372). See also note on 'azurn,' l. 893.

346. whistle ... lodge, *i.e.* the sound of the shepherd calling his dog by whistling. Or it may be used in the same sense as in *L'Alleg.* 63, "the ploughman *whistles* o'er the furrowed land."

347. Count ... dames: comp. *L'Alleg.* 52, "the cock ... Stoutly struts his *dames* before"; 114, "Ere the first cock his matin rings." Grammatically, 'count' (infinitive) forms with 'cock' the complex object of 'might hear.'

349. innumerous, innumerable (Lat. *innumerus*). Comp. *Par. Lost*, vii. 455, *"Innumerous* living creatures"; ix. 1089.

350. hapless, unfortunate. Many words, such as happy, lucky, fortunate, etc., which strictly refer to a person's hap or chance, whether good or bad, have become restricted to good hap: in order to give them an unfavourable meaning a negative prefix or suffix is necessary.

With reference to the word *fortune*, Max Müller says: "We speak of good and evil fortune, so did the French, and so did the Romans. By itself *fortuna* was taken either in a good or a bad sense, though it generally meant good fortune. Whenever there could be any doubt, the Romans defined *fortuna* by such adjectives as *bona*, *secunda*, *prospera*, for good; *mala* or *adversa* for bad fortune ... *Fortuna* came to mean something like chance."

351. her, herself. On the reflexive use of *her*, see note, l. 163.

352. burs; burrs, prickly seed-vessels of certain plants, *e.g.* the burr-thistle, the burdock (= the burr-dock), etc.

355. leans. As Milton frequently omits the nominative, we may supply *she*: otherwise *leans* would be intransitive and its nominative 'head': see note, l. 715. fraught, freighted, filled. *Freight* is itself a later form of *fraught*: in *Sams. Agon.*, 1075, *fraught* is a noun (Ger. *fracht*, a load). See line 732.

356. What, etc. The ellipses may be supplied thus: "What (shall be done) if (she be) in wild amazement?"

358. savage hunger. 'Hunger' is put by synecdoche for hungry animals.

359. over-exquisite, *i.e.* too curious, over-inquisitive. *Exquisite* is here used in the sense of *inquisitive*; in modern English 'exquisite' has a passive sense only, while 'inquisitive' has an active sense (Lat. *quaero*, to seek): see note, l. 714.

"The dialogue between the two brothers is an amicable contest between fact and philosophy. The younger draws his arguments from common apprehension, and the obvious appearance of things; the elder proceeds on a profounder knowledge, and argues from abstracted principles. Here the difference of their ages is properly made subservient to a contrast of character" (Warton).

360. To cast the fashion, *i.e.* to prejudge the form. 'To cast' was common in the sense of to calculate or compute; see Shakespeare, ii. *Henry IV.* i. 1. 166, "You *cast* the event of war." Some think, however, that the word has here its still more restricted sense as used in astrology, *e.g.* "to *cast* a nativity"; others see in it a reference to the founder's art; and others to medical diagnosis.

361. Grant they be so: a concessive clause = granted that the evils turn out to be what you imagined. The alternative is given in l. 364.

362. What need, etc., *i.e.* why should a man anticipate his hour of sorrow. 'What' = for what (Lat. *quid*): comp. l. 752; also *On Shakespeare*, 6, "*What need'st* thou such weak witness of thy name?" On the verb *need* Abbott, § 297, says: "It is often found with 'what,' where it is sometimes hard to say whether 'what' is an adverb and 'need' a verb, or 'what' an adjective and 'need' a noun. 'What need the bridge much broader than the flood?' *M. Ado*, i. 1. 318; either '*why need* the bridge (be) broader?' or '*what need* is there (that) the bridge (be) broader?'"

363. Compare Hamlet's famous soliloquy, "rather bear those ills we have," etc.; and Pope's *Essay on Man*, "Heaven from all creatures hides the book of fate," etc.

366. to seek, at a loss. Compare *Par. Lost*, viii. 197: "Unpractised, unprepared, and still *to seek*." Bacon, in *Adv. of Learning*, has: "Men bred in learning are perhaps *to seek* in points of convenience."

367. unprincipled in virtue's book, *i.e.* ignorant of the elements of virtue. A principle (Lat. *principium*, beginning) is a fundamental truth; hence the current sense of 'unprincipled,' implying that the man who has no fixed rules of life is the one who will readily fall into evil. Comp. *Sams. Agon.* 760, "wisest and best men ... with goodness *principled*."

368. bosoms, holds within itself. The nom. is 'goodness.' 'Peace' is governed by 'in,' l. 367.

369. As that, etc. This is an adverbial clause of consequence to 'unprincipled'; in modern English such a clause would be introduced by 'that,' and in Elizabethan English either by 'as' or 'that.' Here we have both connectives together. single: see note, l. 204. noise, sound.

370. Not being in danger, *i.e.* she not being in danger: absolute construction. This parenthetical line is equivalent to a conditional clause—'if she be not in danger, the mere want of light and noise need not disquiet her.'

371. constant, steadfast.

372. misbecoming: see note on 'misused,' l. 47. plight, condition. Skeat derives this word from A.S. *pliht*, danger; others connect it with *pledge*. It is distinct from *plight*, l. 301.

373. Virtue could see, etc. The best commentary on this line is in lines 381-5: comp. Spenser: "Virtue gives herself light through darkness for to wade," *F. Q.* i. 1. 12.

375. flat sea: comp. *Lyc.* 98, "level brine": Lat. *aequor*, a flat surface, used of the sea.

376. seeks to, applies herself to. This use of seek is common in the English Bible: see *Deut.* xii. 5, *"unto his habitation shall ye seek"*; *Isaiah*, viii. 19, xi. 10, xix. 3; i. *Kings*, x. 24.

377. her best nurse, Contemplation. The wise man loves contemplation and solitude: comp. *Il Penseroso*, 51, where "the Cherub Contemplation" is the "first and chiefest" of Melancholy's companions. In Sidney's *Arcadia*, "Solitariness" is "the nurse of these contemplations."

378. plumes. Some would read *prunes*, both words being used of a bird's smoothing or trimming its feathers—or (more strictly) picking out damaged feathers. See Skeat's *Dictionary*, and compare Pope's line, "Where Contemplation *prunes* her ruffled wings."

379. various, varied: comp. l. 22. The 'bustle of resort' is in *L'Allegro* the 'busy hum of men.'

380. all to-ruffled. Milton wrote "all to ruffled," which may be interpreted in various ways: (1) all to-ruffled, (2) all too ruffled, (3) all-to ruffled. The first of these is given in the text as it is etymologically correct: *to* is an intensive prefix as in

'to-break' = to break in pieces; 'to-tear' = to tear asunder, etc.; while *all* (= quite) is simply an adverb modifying *to-ruffled*. But about 1500 A.D. this idiom was misunderstood, and the prefix *to* was detached from the verb and either read along with *all* (thus all-to = altogether), or confused with *too* (thus all-to = too too, decidedly too). It is doubtful in which sense Milton used the phrase; like Shakespeare, he may have disregarded its origin. See Morris, § 324; Abbott, §§ 28, 436.

381. He that has light, etc. Comp. *Par. Lost*, i. 254: 'The mind is its own place,' etc.

382. centre, *i.e.* centre of the earth: comp. *Par. Lost* i. 686, "Men also ... Ransacked the *centre*"; and *Hymn Nat.* 162, "The aged Earth ... Shall from the surface to the *centre* shake." Sometimes the word 'centre' was used of the Earth itself, the *fixed* centre of the whole universe according to the Ptolemaic system. The idea here conveyed, however, is not that of immovability (as in *Par. Reg.* iv. 534, "as a *centre* firm") but of utter darkness.

385. his own dungeon: comp. *Sams. Agon.* 156, "Thou art become (O worst imprisonment!) The *dungeon* of thyself."

386. most affects: has the greatest liking for. It now generally denotes rather a feigned than a real liking: comp. *pretend.* Lines 386-392 may be compared with *Il Pens.* 167-174.

393. Hesperian tree. An allusion to the tree on which grew the golden apples of Juno, which were guarded by the Hesperides and the sleepless dragon Ladon. Hence the reference to the 'dragon watch': comp. Tennyson's *Dream of Fair Women*, 255, "Those dragon eyes of anger'd Eleanor Do hunt me, day and night." See also ll. 981-983.

395. unenchanted, superior to all the powers of enchantment, not to be enchanted. Similarly Milton has 'unreproved' for 'not reprovable,' 'unvalued' for 'invaluable,' etc.; and Shakespeare has 'unavoided' for 'inevitable,' 'imagined' for 'imaginable,' etc. Abbott (§ 375) says: The passive participle is often used to signify, not that which *was* and *is*, but that which *was* and therefore *can be hereafter*; in other words *-ed* is used for *-able*.

396. Compare Chaucer, *Doctor's Tale*, 44, "She flowered in virginity, With all humility and abstinence."

398. unsunned, hidden. Comp. *Cym.* ii. 5. 13, "As chaste as *unsunned* snow"; *F. Q.* ii. 7, "Mammon . . . *Sunning* his treasure hoar."
400. as bid me hope, etc. The construction is, 'as (you may) bid me (to) hope (that) Danger will wink on Opportunity and (that Danger will) let a single helpless maiden pass uninjured.'
401. Danger will wink on, etc., *i.e.* danger will shut its eyes to an opportunity. To *wink on* or *wink at* is to connive, to refuse to see something: comp. *Macbeth*, i. 4. 52, "The eye *wink* at the hand"; *Acts*, xvii. 30. Warton notes a similar argument by Rosalind in *As You Like It*, i. 3. 113: "Beauty provoketh thieves sooner than gold."
403. surrounding. Milton is said to be the first author of any note who uses this word in its current sense of 'encompassing,' which it has acquired through a supposed connection with *round*. Shakespeare does not use it. Its original sense is 'to overflow' (Lat. *superundare*).
404. it recks me not, *i.e.* I do not heed: an impersonal use of the old verb *reck* (A.S. *récan*, to care). Comp. *Lyc.* 122, "What *recks* it them."
405. dog them both, *i.e.* follow closely upon night and loneliness. Comp. *All's Well*, iii. 4. 15, "death and danger *dogs* the heels of worth."
407. unownèd, *i.e.* 'thinking her to be unowned,' or 'as if unowned.' Milton thus, as in Latin, frequently condenses a clause into a participle.
408. infer, reason, argue. This use of the word is obsolete. See Shakespeare, iii. *Hen. VI.* ii. 2. 44, "*Inferring* arguments of mighty force"; *K. John*, iii. 1. 213, "Need must needs *infer* this principle": also *Par. Lost*, viii. 91, "great or bright *infers* not excellence."
409. without all doubt, *i.e.* beyond all doubt: a Latinism = *sine omni dubitatione.*
411. arbitrate the event, judge of the result. The meaning is 'Where the result depends equally upon circumstances to be hoped and to be dreaded I incline to hope.'
413. squint suspicion. Compare Quarles: "Heart-gnawing Hatred, and squint-eyed Suspicion." To look askance or sideways frequently indicates suspicion.
419. if Heaven gave it, *i.e.* even *although* Heaven gave it.

420. 'Tis chastity. "The passage which begins here and ends at line 475 is a concentrated expression of the moral of the whole Masque, and an exposition also of a cardinal idea of Milton's philosophy" (Masson).

421. clad in complete steel, *i.e.* completely armed; comp. *Hamlet*, i. 4. 52, where the phrase occurs. The accent is on the first syllable.

422. quivered nymph. The chaste Diana of the Romans was armed with bow and quiver; and Shakespeare makes virginity "Diana's livery." So in Spenser, Belphoebe, the personification of Chastity, has "at her back a bow and quiver gay." 'Quivered' is the Latin *pharetrata*.

423. trace, traverse, track. unharboured, affording no shelter. Radically, a harbour is a lodging or shelter.

424. Infámous, having a bad name, ill-famed: a Latinism. The word now implies disgrace or guilt. It is here accented on the penult.

425. sacred rays: comp. l. 782.

426. bandite or mountaineer. 'Bandite' (in Shakespeare *bandetto*, and now *bandit*) is borrowed from the Italian *bandito*, outlawed or *banned*. 'Mountaineer,' here used in a bad sense. In modern English it has reverted to its original sense—a dweller in mountains. The dwellers in mountains are often fierce and readily become freebooters: hence the changes of meaning. See *Temp*. iii. 3. 44, "Who would believe that there were *mountaineers* Dew-lapp'd like bulls"; also *Cym*. iv. 2. 120, "Who called me traitor, *mountaineer*."

428. very desolation. Very (as an adj.) = true or real and may be traced to Lat. *verus* = true: comp. l. 646.

429. shagged ... shades. 'Shagged' is rugged or shaggy, and 'horrid' is probably used in the Latin sense of 'rough': see note, l. 38.

430. unblenched, undaunted, unflinching. This word, sometimes confounded with 'unblanched,' is from *blench*, a causal of *blink*.

431. Be it not: a conditional clause = on condition that it be not.

432. Some say, etc. Compare *Hamlet*, i. 1. 158:

"Some say that, ever against that season comes
Wherein our Saviour's birth is celebrated,

>The bird of dawning singeth all night long:
>And then, they say, no spirit dares stir abroad."

433. In fog or fire, etc. Comp. *Il Pens.* 93, "those demons that are found In fire, air, flood, or underground": an allusion to the different orders and powers of demons as accepted in the Middle Ages. Burton, in his *Anat. of Mel.*, quotes from a writer who thus enumerates the kinds of sublunary spirits—"fiery, aerial, terrestrial, watery, and subterranean, besides fairies, satyrs, nymphs, etc."

434. meagre hag, lean witch. *Hag* is from A.S. *haegtesse*, a prophetess or witch. Comp. *Par. Lost*, ii. 662; *M. W. of W.* iv. 2. 188, "Come down, you witch, you *hag.*" unlaid ghost, unpacified or wandering spirit. It was a superstition that ghosts left the world of spirits and wandered on the earth from the hour of curfew (see *Temp.* v. 1. 40; *King Lear*, iii. 4. 120, "This is the foul fiend Flibbertigibbet; he begins at curfew," etc.) until "the first cock his matin rings" *(L'Alleg.* 14). 'Curfew' (Fr. *couvre-feu* = fire-cover), the bell that was rung at eight or nine o'clock in the evening as a signal that all fires and lights were to be extinguished.

436. swart faery of the mine. In Burton's *Anat. of Mel.* we read, "Subterranean devils are as common as the rest, and do as much harm. Olaus Magnus makes six kinds of them, some bigger, some less. These are commonly seen about mines of metals," etc. Warton quotes from an old writer: "Pioneers or diggers for metal do affirm that in many mines there appear strange shapes and spirits who are apparelled like unto the labourers in the pit." 'Swart' (also *swarty*, *swarth*, and *swarthy*) here means black: in Scandinavian mythology these subterranean spirits were called the *Svartalfar*, or black elves. Comp. *Lyc.* 138, "the *swart* star," where 'swart' = swart making.

438. Do ye believe. *Ye* is properly a second person plural, but (like *you*) is frequently used as a singular: for examples, see Abbott, § 236.

439. old schools of Greece. The brother now turns for his arguments from the mediaeval mythology of Northern Europe to the ancient legends of Greece.

440. to testify, to bear witness to: comp. l. 248, 421.

441. Dian. Diana was the huntress among the immortals: she was insensible to the bolts of Cupid, *i.e.* to the power of love. She was the protectress of the flocks and game from beasts of prey, and at the same time was believed to send plagues and sudden deaths among men and animals. Comp. the song to Cynthia (Diana) in *Cynthia's Revels*, v. 1, "Queen and huntress, chaste and fair," etc.

442. silver-shafted queen. The epithet is applicable to Diana both as huntress and goddess of the moon: as the former she bore arrows which were frequently called *shafts*, and as the latter she bore shafts or rays of light. *Shaft* is etymologically 'a *shaven* rod.' In Chaucer, *C. T.* 1364, 'shaft' = arrow.

443. brinded lioness. 'Brinded' = brindled or streaked. Comp. "*brinded* cat," *Macb.* iv. 1. 1: *brind* is etymologically connected with *brand*.

444. mountain-pard, *i.e.* panther or other spotted wild beast. *Pard*, originally a Persian word, is common in the compounds leo-*pard* and camelo-*pard*.

445. frivolous ... Cupid. See the speech of Oberon, *M. N. D.* ii. 1. 65. The epithet 'frivolous' applies to Cupid in his lower character as the wanton god of sensual love, not in his character as the fair Eros who unites all the discordant elements of the universe: see note, l. 1004.

447. snaky-headed Gorgon shield. Medusa was one of the three Gorgons, frightful beings, whose heads were covered with hissing serpents, and who had wings, brazen claws, and huge teeth. Whoever looked at Medusa was turned into stone, but Perseus, by the aid of enchantment, slew her. Minerva (Athene) placed the monster's head in the centre of her shield, which confounded Cupid: see *Par. Lost*, ii. 610.

449. freezed, froze. The adjective 'congealed' is used proleptically, the meaning being 'froze into a stone so that it was congealed.'

450. But, except: a preposition.

451. dashed, confounded: this meaning of the word is obsolete.

452. blank awe: the awe of one amazed. Comp. the phrase, 'blank astonishment,' and see *Par. Lost*, ix. 890.

454. so, *i.e.* chaste.

455. liveried angels lackey her, *i.e.* ministering angels attend her. So, in *L'Alleg.* 62, "the clouds in thousand *liveries* dight"; a servant's livery being the distinctive dress *delivered* to him by his master. 'Lackey,' to wait upon, from 'lackey' (or lacquey), a footboy, who runs by the side of his master. The word is here used in a good sense, without implying servility (as in *Ant. and Cleop.* i. 4. 46, *"lackeying* the varying tide"). 'Her': the soul. Milton is fond of the feminine personification: see line 396.

457. vision: a trisyllable.

458. no gross ear. See notes, l. 112 and 997.

459. oft converse, frequent communion. *Oft* is here used adjectively: this use is common in the English Bible, *e.g.* i. *Tim.* v. 23, "thine *often* infirmities."

460. Begin to cast ... turns. 'Begin' is subjunctive; 'turns' is indicative: the latter may be used to convey greater certainty and vividness.

461. temple of the mind, *i.e.* the body. This metaphor is common: see Shakespeare, *Temp.* i. 2. 57, "There's nothing ill can dwell in such a *temple*"; and the Bible, *John*, ii. 21, "He spake of the *temple* of his body."

462. the soul's essence. As if, by a life of purity, the body gradually became spiritualised, and therefore partook of the soul's immortality.

465. most, above all.

467. soul grows clotted. This doctrine is expounded in Plato's *Phaedo*, in a conversation between Socrates and Cebes:

Socrates (speaking of the pure soul). That soul, I say, herself invisible, departs to the invisible world—to the divine and immortal and rational: thither arriving, she is secure of bliss, and is released from the error and folly of men, their fears and wild passions and all other human ills, and for ever dwells, as they say of the initiated, in company with the gods. Is not this true, Cebes?

Cebes. Yes; beyond a doubt.

Soc. But the soul which has been polluted, and is impure at the time of her departure, and is the companion and servant of the body always, and is in love with and fascinated by the body and by the desires and pleasures of the body, until she is led to believe that the truth only exists in a bodily form, which a man may touch and see and taste, and use for the purposes of his lusts—the soul, I mean, accustomed to hate and fear and avoid the intellectual principle, which to the bodily eye is dark and invisible and can be attained only by philosophy;—do you suppose that such a soul will depart pure and unalloyed?

Ceb. That is impossible.

Soc. She is held fast by the corporeal, which the continual association and constant care of the body have wrought into her nature.

Ceb. Very true.

Soc. And this corporeal element, my friend, is heavy and weighty and earthy, and is that element by which such a soul is depressed and dragged down again into the visible world, because she is afraid of the invisible and of the world below— prowling about tombs and sepulchres, in the neighbourhood of which, as they tell us, are seen certain ghostly apparitions of souls which have not departed pure, but are cloyed with sight and therefore visible.

Ceb. That is very likely, Socrates.

Soc. Yes, that is very likely, Cebes; and these must be the souls, not of the good, but of the evil, who are compelled to wander about such places in payment of the penalty of their former evil way of life; and they continue to wander until through the craving after the corporeal which never leaves them, they are imprisoned finally in another body. And they may be supposed to find their prisons in the same natures which they have had in their former lives.

Further on in the same dialogue, Socrates says:

Each pleasure and pain is a sort of nail which nails and rivets the soul to the body, until she becomes like the body, and believes that to be true which the body affirms to be true; and from agreeing with the body, and having the same delights, she is obliged to have the same habits and haunts, and is not likely ever to be pure at her departure, but is always infected by the body.—*Extracted from Jowett's Translation of the Dialogues.*

468. imbodies and imbrutes, *i.e.* becomes materialised and brutish. *Imbody*, ordinarily used as a transitive verb, is here intransitive. *Imbrute* (said to have been coined by Milton) is also intransitive; in *Par. Lost*, ix. 166, it is transitive. The use of the word may

have been suggested by the *Phaedo*, where the souls of the wicked are said to "find their prisons in the same natures which they have had in their former lives," those of gluttons and drunkards passing into asses and animals of that sort.

469. divine property. In his prose works Milton calls the soul 'that divine particle of God's breathing': comp. Horace, *Sat.* ii. 2. 79, "affigit humo *divinae particulam aurae*"; and Plato's *Phaedo*, "'The soul resembles the divine, and the body the mortal."

470. gloomy shadows damp: see note, l. 207.

471. charnel-vaults, burial vaults. 'Charnel' (O.F. *charnel*, Lat. *carnalis*; *caro*, flesh): comp. 'carnal,' l. 474.

473. As loth, etc. The construction is: 'As (being) loth to leave the body that it loved, and (as having) linked itself to a degenerate and degraded state.' it: by syntax this pronoun refers to 'shadows,' or (in thought) *'such* shadow.' It seems best, however, to connect it with 'soul,' line 467.

474. sensualty. The modern form of the word is *sensuality*.

475. degenerate and degraded: the former because 'imbodied,' the latter because 'imbruted.'

476. divine Philosophy, *i.e.* such philosophy as is to be found in "the divine volume of Plato" (as Milton has called it).

477. crabbed, sour or bitter: comp. crab-apple. *Crab* (a shell-fish) and *crab* (a kind of apple) are radically connected, both conveying the idea of scratching or pinching (Skeat).

478. Apollo's lute: Apollo being the god of song and music. Comp. *Par. Reg.* i. 478-480; *L. L. L.* iv. 3. 342, "as sweet and musical As bright *Apollo's lute*, strung with his hair."

479. nectared sweets. Nectar (Gk. +nektar+, the drink of the gods) is repeatedly used by Milton to express the greatest sweetness: see l. 838; *Par. Lost*, iv. 333, "Nectarine fruits"; v. 306, 426.

482. Methought: see note, l. 171. what should it be? This is a direct question about a past event, and means 'What was it likely to be?' "It seems to increase the emphasis of the interrogation, since a doubt about the past (time having been given for investigation) implies more perplexity than a doubt about the future" (Abbott, § 325). For certain, *i.e.* for certain truth, certainly.

483. night-foundered; benighted, lost in the darkness. Radically, 'to founder' is to go to the bottom (Fr. *fondrer*; Lat. *fundus*, the

bottom), hence applied to ships; it is also applied to horses sinking in a slough. The compound is Miltonic (see *Par. Lost*, i. 204), and is sometimes stigmatised as meaningless; on the contrary, it is very expressive, implying that the brothers are swallowed up in night and have lost their way. 'Founder' is here used in the secondary sense of 'to be lost' or 'to be in distress.'

484. neighbour. An adjective, as in line 576, and frequently in Shakespeare. Neighbour = nigh-boor, *i.e.* a peasant dwelling near.

487. Best draw: we had best draw our swords.

489. Defence is a good cause, etc., *i.e.* 'in defending ourselves we are engaged in a good cause, and may Heaven be on our side.'

490. That hallo. We are to understand that the Attendant Spirit has halloed just before entering; this is shown by the stage-direction given in the edition of *Comus* printed by Lawes in 1637: *He hallos; the Guardian Dæmon hallos again, and enters in the habit of a shepherd.*

491. you fall, etc., *i.e.* otherwise you will fall on our swords.

493. sure: see note, l. 246.

494. Thyrsis, Like Lycidas, this name is common in pastoral poetry. In Milton's *Epitaphium Damonis* it stands for Milton himself; in *Comus* it belongs to Lawes, who now receives additional praise for his musical genius. In lines 86-88 the compliment is enforced by alliterative verses, and here by the aid of rhyme (495-512). Masson thinks that the poet, having spoken of the madrigals of Thyrsis, may have introduced this rhymed passage in order to prolong the feeling of Pastoralism by calling up the cadence of known English pastoral poems.

495. sweetened ... dale; poetical exaggeration or hyperbole, implying that fragrant flowers became even more fragrant from Thyrsis' music.

496. huddling. This conveys the two ideas of hastening and crowding: comp. Horace, *Ars Poetica*, 19, "Et *properantis* aquae per amoenos ambitus agros." madrigal: a pastoral or shepherd's song (Ital. *mandra*, a flock): such compositions, then in favour, had been made by Lawes and by Milton's father.

497. swain: a word of common use in pastoral poetry. It denotes strictly a peasant or, more correctly, a young man: comp. the compounds boat-*swain*, cox-*swain*. See *Arc.* 26, "Stay, gentle *swains*," etc.

499. pent, penned, participle of *pen*, to shut up (A.S. *pennan*, which is connected with *pin*, seen in *pin*-fold, l. 7). forsook: a form of the past tense used for the participle.

501. and his next joy, *i.e.* 'and (thou), his next joy'—words addressed to the second brother.

502. trivial toy, ordinary trifle. The phrase seems redundant, but 'trivial' may here be used in the strict sense of common or well-known. Compare *Il Pens.* 4, "fill the fixed mind with all your *toys*"; and Burton's *Anat. of Mel.*, "complain of *toys*, and fear without a cause."

503. stealth of, things stolen by.

506. To this my errand, etc., *i.e.* in comparison with this errand of mine and the anxiety it involved. 'To' = in comparison with; an idiom common in Elizabethan English, *e.g.* "There is no woe *to* this correction," *Two Gent.* ii. 4. 138. See Abbott, § 187.

508. How chance. *Chance* is here a verb followed by a substantive clause: 'how does it chance that,' etc. This idiom is common in Shakespeare (Abbott, § 37), where it sometimes has the force of an adverb (= perchance): compare *Par. Lost*, ii. 492: "If chance the radiant sun, with farewell sweet," etc.

509. sadly, seriously. Radically, sad = sated or full (A.S. *saed*); hence the two meanings, 'serious' and 'sorrowful,' the former being common in Spenser, Bacon, and Shakespeare. Comp. 'some *sad* person of known judgment' (Bacon); *Romeo and Jul.* i. 1. 205, "Tell me in *sadness*, who is that you love"; *Par. Lost*, vi. 541, "settled in his face I see *Sad* resolution." See also Swinburne's *Miscellanies* (1886), page 170.

510. our neglect, *i.e.* neglect on our part.

511. Ay me! Comp. *Lyc.* 56, "Ay me! I fondly dream"; 154. This exclamatory phrase = ah me! Its form is due to the French *aymi* = alas, for me! and has no connection with *ay* or *aye* = yes. In this line *true* rhymes with *shew*: comp. *youth* and *shew'th*, *Sonnet on his having arrived at the age of twenty-three*.

512. Prithee. A familiar fusion of *I pray thee*, sometimes written 'pr'ythee.' Lines 495-512 form nine rhymed couplets.

513. ye: a dative. See note on l. 216.

514. shallow. Comp. *Son.* i. 6, "*shallow* cuckoo's bill," xii*a*. 12; *Arc.* 41, "*shallow*-searching Fame."

515. sage poets. Homer and Virgil are meant; both of these mention the chimera. Milton *(Par. Lost*, iii. 19) afterwards speaks of himself as "taught by the heavenly Muse." Comp. *L'Alleg.* 17; *Il Pens.* 117, "great bards besides In sage and solemn tunes have sung."

516. storied, related: 'To story' is here used actively: the past participle is frequent in the sense of 'bearing a story or picture'; *Il Pens.* 159, "storied windows"; Gray's *Elegy*, 41, "storied urn"; Tennyson's "storied walls." *Story* is an abbreviation of *history*.

517. Chimeras, monsters. Comp. the sublime passage in *Par. Lost*, ii. 618-628. The Chimera was a fire-breathing monster, with the head of a lion, the tail of a dragon, and the body of a goat. It was slain by Bellerophon. As a common name 'chimera' is used by Milton to denote a terrible monster, and is now current (in an age which rejects such fabulous creatures) in the sense of a wild fancy; hence the adj. *chimerical* = wild or fanciful. enchanted isles, *e.g.* those of Circe and Calypso, mentioned in the *Odyssey*.

518. rifted rocks: rifted = riven. Orpheus, in search of Eurydice, entered the lower world through the rocky jaws of Taenarus, a cape in the south of Greece (see Virgil *Georg.* iv. 467, *Taenarias fauces*); here also Hercules emerged from Hell with the captive Cerberus.

519. such there be. See note on l. 12 for this indicative use of *be*.

520. navel, centre, inmost recess. Shakespeare *(Cor.* iii. 1. 123) speaks of the 'navel of the state'; and in Greek Calypso's island was 'the navel of the sea,' while Apollo's temple at Delphi was 'the navel of the earth.'

521. Immured, enclosed. Here used generally: radically it = shut up within walls (Lat. *murus*, a wall).

523. witcheries, enchantments.

526. murmurs. The incantations or spells of evil powers were sung or murmured over the doomed object; sometimes they were muttered (as here) over the enchanted food or drink prepared for the victim. Comp. l. 817 and *Arc.* 60, "With puissant words and *murmurs* made to bless."

529. unmoulding reason's mintage charactered, *i.e.* defacing those signs of a rational soul that are stamped on the human face. The figure is taken from the process of melting down coins in order to restamp them. 'Charactered': here used in its primary sense (Gk. +charaktêr+, an engraven or stamped mark), as in the phrase 'printed characters.' The word is here accented on the second syllable; in modern English on the first.

531. crofts that brow = crofts that overhang. Croft = a small field, generally adjoining a house. Brow = overhang: comp. *L'Alleg.* 8, "low-browed rocks."

532. bottom glade: the glade below. The word *bottom*, however, is frequent in Shakespeare in the sense of 'valley'; hence 'bottom glade' might be interpreted 'glade in the valley.'

533. monstrous rout; see note on the stage-direction after l. 92. Comp. 'the bottom of the monstrous world,' *Lyc.* 158. In *Aen.* vii. 15, we read that when Aeneas sailed past Circe's island he heard "the growling noise of lions in wrath, . . . and shapes of huge wolves fiercely howling."

534. stabled wolves, wolves in their dens. *Stable* (= a standing-place) is used by Milton in the general sense of abode, *e.g.* in *Par. Lost*, xi. 752, "sea-monsters whelped and *stabled*." Comp. "Stable for camels," *Ezek.* xxv. 5, and the Latin *stabulum*, *Aen.* vi. 179, *stabula alta ferarum*.

535. Hecate: see l. 135.

536. bowers: see note, l. 45.

539. unweeting; unwitting, unknowing. This spelling is found in Spenser's *Faerie Queene*, both in the compounds and in the simple verb *weet*, a corruption of *wit* (A.S. *witan*, to know). Compare *Par. Reg.* i. 126, "*unweeting*, he fulfilled The purposed counsel." *Sams. Agon.* 1680; Chaucer, *Doctor's Tale*, "Virginius came *to weet* the judge's will."

540. by then, *i.e.* by the time when. The demonstrative adverb thus implies a relative adverb: comp. the Greek, where the demonstrative is generally omitted, though in Homer occasionally the demonstrative alone is used. Another rendering is to make line 540 parenthetical.

542. knot-grass. A grass with knotted or jointed stem: some, however, suppose marjoram to be intended here. dew-besprent, *i.e.* besprinkled with dew: comp. *Lyc.* 29. *Be* is an

intensive prefix; *sprent* is connected with M.E. *sprengen*, to scatter, of which *sprinkle* is the frequentative form.

543. sat me down: see note, l. 61.

544. canopied, and interwove. Comp. *M. N. D.* ii. 2. 49, 'I know a bank,' etc. In sense 'canopied' refers to 'bank,' and 'interwove' to 'ivy.' There are two forms of the past participle of *weave*, viz. *wove* and *woven*: see *Arc.* 47.

545. flaunting, showy, garish. In *Lyc.* 146, the poet first wrote 'garish columbine,' then 'well-attired woodbine.'

547. meditate ... minstrelsy, *i.e.* to sing a pastoral song: comp. *Lyc.* 32. 66. *To meditate the muse* is a Virgilian phrase: see *Ecl.* i. and vi. The Lat. *meditor* has the meaning of 'to apply one's self to,' and does not mean merely to ponder.

548. had, should have: comp. l. 394. ere a close, *i.e.* before he had finished his song (Masson). *Close* occurs in the technical sense of 'the final cadence of a piece of music.'

549. wonted: see note, l. 332.

550. barbarous: comp. *Son.* xii. 3, "a *barbarous* noise environs me Of owls and cuckoos, etc."

551. listened them. The omission of *to* after verbs of hearing is frequent in Shakespeare and others: comp. "To listen our purpose"; "List a brief tale"; "hearken the end"; etc. (see Abbott, § 199). 'Them': this refers to the *sounds* implied in 'dissonance.'

552. unusual stop. This refers to what happened at l. 145, and the "soft and solemn-breathing sound" to l. 230.

553. drowsy frighted, *i.e.* drowsy and frighted. The noise of Comus's rout is here supposed to have kept the horses of night awake and in a state of drowsy agitation until the sudden calm put an end to their uneasiness. In Milton's corrected MS. we read 'drowsy flighted,' where the two words are not co-ordinate epithets but must be regarded as expressing one idea = flying drowsily; to express this some insert a hyphen. Comp. 'dewy-feathered,' *Il Pens.* 146, and others of Milton's remarkable compound adjectives. The reading in the text is that of the printed editions of 1637, '45, and '73.

554. Sleep (or Night) is represented as drawn by horses in a chariot with its curtains closely drawn. Comp. *Macbeth*, ii. 1. 51, "curtained sleep."

555. 'The lady's song rose into the air so sweetly and imperceptibly that silence was taken unawares and so charmed that she would gladly have renounced her nature and existence for ever if her place could always be filled by such music.' Comp. *Par. Lost*, iv. 604, "She all night long her amorous descant sung; *Silence was pleased*"; also Jonson's *Vision of Delight*:

"Yet let it like an odour rise
To all the senses here,
And fall like sleep upon their eyes,
Or music in their ear."

558. took, taken. Comp. l. 256 for a similar use of *take*, and compare 'forsook,' line 499, for the form of the word.

560. Still, always. This use of *still* is frequent in Elizabethan writers (Abbott, § 69). I was all ear. Warton notes this expressive idiom (still current) in Drummond's 'Sonnet to the Nightingale,' and in *Tempest*, iv. 1. 59, "all eyes." *All* is an attribute of *I*.

561. create a soul, etc., *i.e.* breathe life even into the dead: comp. *L'Alleg.* 144. Warton supposes that Milton may have seen a picture in an old edition of Quarles' *Emblems*, in which "a soul in the figure of an infant is represented within the ribs of a skeleton, as in its prison." *Rom.* vii. 24, "Who shall deliver me out of the body of this death?"

565. harrowed, distracted, torn as by a *harrow*. This is probably the meaning, but there is a verb 'harrow' corrupted from 'harry,' to subdue; hence some read "harried with grief and fear."

567. How sweet ... how near. This sentence contains two exclamations: this is a Greek construction. In English the idiom is "How sweet ... *and* how near," etc. We may, however, render the line thus: "How sweet ..., how near the deadly snare *is*!"

568. lawns. 'Lawn' is always used by Milton to denote an open stretch of grassy ground, whereas in modern usage it is applied generally to a smooth piece of grass-grown land in front of a house. The origin of the word is disputed, but it seems radically to denote 'a clear space'; it is said to be cognate with *llan* used as a prefix in the names of certain Welsh towns, *e.g.* Llandaff, Llangollen. In Chaucer it takes the form launde.

569. often trod by day, which I have often trod by day, and therefore know well.

570. mine ear: see note, l. 171.
571. wizard. Here used in contempt, like many other words with the suffix *-ard*, or *-art*, as braggart, sluggard, etc. Milton occasionally, however, uses the word merely in the sense of magician or magical, without implying contempt: see *Lyc.* 55, "Deva spreads her *wizard* stream."
572. certain signs: see l. 644.
574. aidless: an obsolete word. See Trench's *English Past and Present* for a list of about 150 words in *-less*, all now obsolete: comp. l. 92, note. wished: wished for. Comp. l. 950 for a similar transitive use of the verb.
575. such two: two persons of such and such description.
577. durst not stay. *Durst* is the old past tense of *dare*, and is used as an auxiliary: the form *dared* is much more modern, and may be used as an independent verb.
578. sprung: see note, l. 256.
579. till I had found. The language is extremely condensed here, the meaning being, 'I began my flight, and continued to run till I *had found* you'; the pluperfect tense is used because the speaker is looking back upon his meeting with the brothers after completing a long narration of the circumstances that led up to it. If, however, 'had found' be regarded as a subjunctive, the meaning is, 'I began my flight, and determined to continue it until I had found *(i.e.* should have found) you.' Comp. Abbott § 361.
581. triple knot, a three-fold alliance of Night, Shades, and Hell.
584. "This confidence of the elder brother in favour of the final efficacy of virtue, holds forth a very high strain of philosophy, delivered in as high strains of eloquence and poetry" (Warton). And Todd adds: "Religion here gave energy to the poet's strains."
585. safely, confidently. period, sentence.
586. for me, *i.e.* for my part, so far as I am concerned: see note, l. 602.
588. Which erring men call Chance. 'Erring' belongs to the predicate; "which men erroneously call Chance." Comp. Pope, *Essay on Man*:

"All nature is but art, unknown to thee;
All chance, direction, which thou canst not see."

588. this I hold firm. 'This' is explained by the next line: "this belief, namely, that Virtue may be assailed, etc., I hold firmly."

590. enthralled, enslaved. Comp. l. 1022.

591. which ... harm, which the Evil Power intended to be most harmful.

595-7. Gathered like scum, etc. According to one editor, this image is "taken from the conjectures of astronomers concerning the dark spots which from time to time appear on the surface of the sun's body and after a while disappear again; which they suppose to be the scum of that fiery matter which first breeds it, and then breaks through and consumes it."

598. pillared firmament. The firmament (Lat. *firmus*, firm or solid) is here regarded as the roof of the earth and supported on pillars. The ancients believed the stars to be fixed in the solid firmament: comp. *Par. Reg.* iv. 55; also *Wint. Tale*, ii. l. 100, "If I mistake In those foundations which I build upon, The centre is not big enough to bear A schoolboy's top."

602. for, as regards. let ... girt, though he be surrounded.

603. grisly legions. 'Grisly,' radically the same as *grue-some* = horrible, causing terror. In *Par. Lost*, iv. 821, Satan is called "the grisly king." 'Legions' is here a trisyllable.

604. sooty flag of Acheron. Acheron, at first the name of a river of the lower world, came to be used as a name for the whole of the lower world generally. Todd quotes from P. Fletcher's *Locusts* (1627): "All hell run out and sooty flags display."

605. Harpies and Hydras. The Harpies (lit. 'spoilers') were unclean monsters, being birds with the heads of maidens, with long claws and gaunt faces. *Hydras*, here used as a general name for monstrous water-serpents (Gk. *hyd{=o}r*, water); the name was first given to the nine-headed monster slain by Hercules. See *Son.* xv. 7, "new rebellions raise Their *Hydra* heads"; the epithet 'hydra-headed' being applied to a rebellion, an epidemic, or other evil that seems to gain strength from every endeavour to repress it.

607. return his purchase back, *i.e.* 'give up his spoil,' or (as in the MS.) 'release his new-got prey.' To purchase (Fr. *pour-chasser*) originally meant to pursue eagerly, hence to acquire by fair means or foul: it thus came to mean 'to steal' (as frequently in Spenser, Jonson, and Shakespeare), and 'to buy' (its current

sense). See Trench, *Study of Words*; *Hen. V.* iii. 2. 45, "They will steal anything, and call it *purchase*"; i. *Hen. IV.* ii. 1. 101, "thou shalt have share in our *purchase*."

609. venturous, ready to venture. See note, l. 79.

610. yet, nevertheless. The meaning is: 'Though thy courage is useless, *yet* I love it.' emprise: an obsolete form (common in Spenser) of *enterprise*. It is literally that which is undertaken; hence 'readiness to undertake'; hence 'daring.'

611. can do thee little stead, *i.e.* can help thee little. *Stead*, both as noun and verb, is obsolete except in certain phrases, *e.g.* 'to stand in good stead,' and in composition, *e.g. stead*fast, home*stead*, in*stead*, Hamp*stead*, etc. Its strict sense is place or position: comp. *Il Pens.* 3, "How little you *bested*."

612. Far other arms, *i.e.* very different arms. 'Other' has here its radical sense of 'different,' and can therefore be modified by an adverb.

615. unthread, loosen. Comp. *Temp.* iv. 1. 259, "Go charge my goblins that they grind their joints With dry convulsions, shorten up their sinews With aged cramps."

617. As to make this relation, *i.e.* as to be able to tell this.

619. a certain shepherd lad. This is supposed to refer to Charles Diodati, Milton's dearest friend, to whom he addressed his 1st and 6th elegies, and after whose death he wrote the touching poem *Epitaphium Damonis*, in which he alludes to his friend's medical and botanical skill:

> "There thou shalt cull me simples, and shalt teach
> Thy friend the name and healing powers of each."
> *(Cowper's translation.)*

620. Of small regard to see to: in colloquial English, 'not much to look at.' This is an old idiom: comp. Greek +kalos idein+: see English Bible, "goodly to look to," i. *Sam.* xvi. 12; *Ezek.* xxiii. 15; *Jer.* xlvii. 3.

621. virtuous, of healing power: see note, l. 165. Comp. *Il Pens.* 113, "the virtuous ring and glass."

623. beg me sing: see note, l. 304.

625. ecstasy: see note, l. 261. The Greek *ekstasis* = standing out of one's self.

626. scrip, wallet.
627. simples, medicinal herbs. 'Simple' (Lat. *simplicem*, 'one-fold,' 'not compound') was used of a single ingredient in a medicine; hence its popular use in the sense of 'herb' or 'drug.'
630. me, *i.e.* for me: the ethic dative.
633. bore. The nom. of this verb is, in sense, some such word as the plant or the root.
634. unknown and like esteemed: known and esteemed to a like extent, *i.e.* in both cases not at all. *Like* here corresponds to the prefix *un* in *unknown*. On the description of the plant, see Introduction, reference to Ascham's *Scholemaster*.
635. clouted shoon, patched shoes. The expression is found in Shakespeare, ii. *Hen. VI.* iv. 2. 195, "Spare none but such as go in *clouted shoon*"; *Cym.* iv. 2. 214, "put My *clouted brogues* from off my feet, whose rudeness Answer'd my steps too loud": see examples in Mayhew and Skeat's *M. E. Dictionary*. There are instances, however, of *clout* in the sense of a plate of iron fastened on the sole of a shoe. In either sense of the word 'clouted shoon' would be heavy and coarse. *Shoon* is an old plural (O.E. *scon*); comp. *hosen*, *eyen* (= eyes), *dohtren* (= daughters), *foen* (= foes), etc.
636. more med'cinal, of greater virtue. The line may be scanned thus: And yet | more med | 'cinal is | it than | that Mo | ly. Moly. When Ulysses was approaching the abode of Circe he was met by Hermes, who said: "Come then, I will redeem thee from thy distress, and bring deliverance. Lo, take this herb of virtue, and go to the dwelling of Circe, that it may keep from thy head the evil day. And I will tell thee all the magic sleight of Circe. She will mix thee a potion and cast drugs into the mess; but not even so shall she be able to enchant thee; so helpful is this charmed herb that I shall give thee ... Therewith the slayer of Argos gave me the plant that he had plucked from the ground, and he showed me the growth thereof. It was black at the root, but the flower was like to milk. *Moly* the gods call it, but it is hard for mortal men to dig; howbeit with the gods all things are possible" *(Odyssey*, x. 280, etc., *Butcher and Lang's translation*). In his first Elegy Milton alludes to Mōly as the counter-charm to the spells of Circe: see also Tennyson's *Lotos-Eaters*, "beds of amaranth and *moly*."

638. He called it Hæmony. *He* is the shepherd lad of line 619. *Haemony*: Milton invents the plant, both name and thing. But the adjective *Haemonian* is used, in Latin poetry as = *Thessalian*, Haemonia being the old name of Thessaly. And as Thessaly was regarded as a land of magic, 'Haemonian' acquired the sense of 'magical' (see Ovid, *Met.* vii 264, *"Haemonia* radices valle resectas," etc.), and Milton's Haemony is simply "the magical plant." Coleridge supposes that by the prickles and gold flower of the plant Milton signified the sorrows and triumph of the Christian life.

639. sovran use: see note, l. 41. The use of this adjective with charms, medicines, or remedies of any kind was so very common that the word came to imply 'all-healing,' 'supremely efficacious'; see *Cor.* ii. 1. 125, "The most *sovereign* prescription in Galen."

640. mildew blast: comp. *Arc.* 48-53, *Ham.* iii. 4. 64, "Here is your husband; Like a *mildew'd* ear *Blasting* his wholesome brother." A mildew blast is one giving rise to that kind of blight called mildew (A.S. meledeáw, honey-dew), it being supposed that the prevalence of dry east winds was favourable to its formation.

642. pursed it up, etc., *i.e.* put it in my wallet, though I did not attach much importance to it. little reckoning: comp. *Lyc.* 116, where the very same phrase occurs.

643. Till now that. Here *that* = when, the clause introduced by it being explanatory of *now* (see Abbott, § 284).

646-7. Entered ... came off. 'I entered into the very midst of his treacherous enchantments, and yet escaped.' *Lime-twigs* = snares; in allusion to the practice of catching birds by means of twigs smeared with a viscous substance (called on that account 'birdlime'). Shakespeare makes repeated allusion to this practice: see *Macbeth*, iv. 2. 34; *Two Gent.* ii. 2. 68; ii. *Hen. VI.* i. 3. 91; etc.

649. necromancer's hall. Warton supposes that Milton here thought of a magician's castle which has an enchanted hall invaded by Christian knights, as we read of in the romances of chivalry. *Necromancer*, lit. one who by magical power can commune with the dead (Gk. +nekros+, a corpse); hence a sorcerer. From confusion of the first syllable with that of the Lat. *niger*, black, the art of necromancy came to be called "the black art."

650. Where if he be, Lat. *ubi si sit*: in English the relative adverb in such cases is best rendered by a conjunction + a demonstrative adverb; thus, *'and* if he be *there.'*

651. brandished blade. Comp. Hermes' advice to Ulysses: "When it shall be that Circe smites thee with her long wand, even then draw thy sharp sword from thy thigh, and spring on her, as one eager to slay her," *Odyssey*, x. break his glass. An imitation of Spenser, who makes Sir Guyon break the golden cup of the enchantress Excess, *F. Q.* i. 12, stanza 56.

652. luscious, delicious. The word is a corruption of *lustious* from O.E. *lust* = pleasure: see note, l. 49.

653. But seize his wand. The force of this injunction is shown by lines 815-819.

654. menace high, violent threat. *High* is thus used in a number of figurative senses, *e.g.* a high wind, a high hand, high passions *(Par. Lost*, ix. 123), high descent, high design, etc.

655. Sons of Vulcan. In the *Aeneid* (Bk. viii. 252) we are told that Cacus, son of Vulcan (the Roman God of Fire), "vomited from his throat huge volumes of smoke" when pursued by Hercules, *"Faucibus ingentem fumum,"* etc.

657. apace; quickly, at a great pace. This word has changed its meaning: in Chaucer it means 'at a foot pace,' *i.e.* slowly. The first syllable is the indefinite article *'a'* = one (Skeat).

658. bear: the subjunctive used optatively (Abbott, § 365). *(Stage Direction)* puts by: puts on one side, refuses. goes about to rise, *i.e.* endeavours to rise. This idiomatic use of *go about* still lingers in the phrase 'to *go about* one's business'; comp. 'to *set about*' anything.

659. but, merely: comp. l. 656. After the conditional clause we have here a verb in the present tense ('are chained'), a construction which well expresses the certainty and immediate action of the sorcerer's spell (see Abbott, § 371).

660. your nerves ... alabaster. Comp. *Tempest*, i. 2. 471-484. Milton has the word alabaster three times, twice incorrectly spelled *alablaster* (in this passage and *Par. Lost*, iv. 544) and once correctly, as now entered in the text *(Par. Reg.* iv. 548). Alabaster is a kind of marble: comp. *On Shak.* 14, "make us *marble* with too much conceiving."

661. or, as Daphne was, etc. The construction is: 'if I merely wave this wand, you (become) a marble statue, or (you become) root-bound, as Daphne was, that fled Apollo.' Milton inserts the adverbial clause in the predicate, which is not unusual; he then adds an attributive clause, which is not usual in English, though common in Greek and Latin. Daphne, an Arcadian goddess, was pursued by Apollo, and having prayed for aid, she was changed into a laurel tree (Gk. +daphnê+): comp. the story of Syrinx and Pan, referred to in *Arc.* 106.

662. fled. Comp. the transitive use of the verb in l. 829, 939, *Son.* xviii. 14, "*fly* the Babylonian woe"; *Sams. Agon.* 1541, "*fly* The sight of this so horrid spectacle."

663. freedom of my mind, etc. Comp. Cowper's noble passage, "He is the freeman whom the truth makes free," etc. *(Task,* v. 733).

665. corporal rind: the body, called in *Il Pens.* 92, "this fleshly nook."

668. here be all. See note, l. 12.

669. fancy can beget: comp. *Il Pens.* 6.

672. cordial julep, heart-reviving drink. *Cordial*, lit. hearty (Lat. *cordi*, stem of *cor*, the heart): *julep*, Persian *gul{=a}b*, rose-water.

673. his = its: see note, l. 96.

674. syrups: Arab, *shar{=a}b*, a drink, wine.

675. that Nepenthes, etc. The allusion is explained by the following lines of the *Odyssey*: "Then Helen, daughter of Zeus, turned to new thoughts. Presently she cast a drug into the wine whereof they drank, a drug to lull all pain and anger, and bring forgetfulness of every sorrow. Whoso should drink a draught thereof, when it is mingled in the bowl, on that day he would let no tear fall down his cheeks, not though his father and his mother died ... Medicines of such virtue and so helpful had the daughter of Zeus, which Polydamna, the wife of Thon, had given her, a woman of Egypt, where earth the grain-giver yields herbs in greatest plenty, many that are healing in the cup, and many baneful" *(Butcher and Lang's translation,* iv. 219-230). 'Nepenthes,' a Greek adj. = sorrow-dispelling (+nê+, privative; +penthos+, grief). It is here used by Milton as the name of an opiate and it is now occasionally used as a general name for drugs that relieve pain.

677. Is of such power, etc.: see note, l. 155. The construction is, 'That Nepenthes is not of such power to stir up joy as this (julep is, nor is it) so friendly to life (nor) so cool to thirst.'

679. Why ... to yourself. Comp. Shakespeare, *Son.* i. 8, "Thyself thy foe, to thy sweet self too cruel."

680. 'Nature gave you your beautiful person to be held in trust on certain conditions, of which the most obligatory is that the body should have refreshment after toil, ease after pain. Yet this very condition you disregard, and deal harshly with yourself by refusing my proferred glass at a time when you are in need of food and rest.' Comp. Shakespeare, *Son.* iv. "Unthrifty loveliness, why dost thou spend Upon thyself thy beauty's legacy," etc.

685. unexempt condition, *i.e.* a condition binding on all and at all times, a law of human nature.

687. mortal frailty, *i.e.* weak mortals: abstract for concrete.

688. That. The antecedent of this relative is *you*, l. 682. See note, l. 2.

689. timely, seasonable. So 'timeless' = unseasonable (Scott's *Marmion*, iii. 223, "gambol rude and *timeless* joke"): comp. *Son.* ii. 8, *"timely*-happy spirits"; and l. 970.

693. Was this ... abode? The verb is singular, because 'cottage' and 'safe abode' convey one idea: see Comus's words, l. 320. Notice also that the past tense is used as referring to the past act of telling.

694. aspects: accent on final syllable.

695. oughly-headed: so spelt in Milton's MS. = ugly-headed. *Ugly* is radically connected with *awe*.

698. with visored falsehood and base forgery. A vizor (also spelt *visor, visard, vizard*) is a mask, "a false face." The allusion is to Comus's disguise: see l. 166. *With* in this line, as in lines 672 and 700, denotes *by means of*.

700. liquorish baits: see note on *baited*, l. 162. 'Liquorish,' by catachresis for *lickerish* = tempting to the appetite, causing one to *lick* one's lips. The student should carefully distinguish the three words *lickerish* (as above), *liquorish* (which is really meaningless) and *liquorice* (= licorice = Lat. *glycyrrhiza*), a plant with a sweet root.

702. treasonous; an obsolete word. The current form 'treasonable' has usually a more restricted sense: Milton and Shakespeare use *treasonous* in the more general sense of *traitorous* (a cognate word). In this line 'offer' = the thing offered.

703. good men ... good things. This noble sentiment Milton has borrowed from Euripides, *Medea*, 618, +Kakou gar andros dôr' onêsin ouk echei+ "the gifts of the bad man are without profit." (Newton).

704. that which is not good, etc. This is Platonic: the soul has a rational principle and an irrational or appetitive, and when the former controls the latter, the desires are for what is good only *(Rep.* iv. 439).

707. budge doctors of the Stoic fur. Budge is lambskin with the wool dressed outwards, worn on the edge of the hoods of bachelors of arts, etc. Therefore, if both *budge* and *fur* be taken literally the line is tautological. But 'budge' has the secondary sense of 'solemn,' like a doctor in his robes; and 'fur' may be used figuratively in the sense of *sect*, just as "the cloth" is used to denote the clergy. The whole phrase would thus be equivalent to 'solemn doctors of the Stoic sect.' It is possible that Milton makes equivocal reference to the two senses of 'budge.'

708. the Cynic tub = the tub of Diogenes the Cynic, here put in contempt for the Cynic school of Greek philosophy, which was the forerunner of the Stoic system. Diogenes, one of the early Cynics, lived in a tub, and was fond of calling himself +ho kyôn+ (the dog).

709. the: here used generically.

711. unwithdrawing. In this participle the termination *-ing* seems almost equivalent to that of the past participle: comp. *"all-obeying* breath" (= obeyed by all), *A. and C.* iii. 13, 77. Nature's gifts are not only full but continuous.

714. all to please ... curious taste. *All* = entirely, here modifies the infinitives please and sate. *Curious* = fastidious: its original sense is 'careful' or 'anxious.' Compare the two senses of *exquisite*, note l. 359.

715. set, *i.e.* she set. The pronominal subject is omitted.

717. To deck: infinitive of purpose.

718. in her own loins, *i.e.* in the bowels of the earth.

719. hutched = stored up, enclosed. *Hutch* is an old word for chest or coffer, chiefly used now in the compound 'rabbit-hutch.'
720. To store her children with, *i.e. wherewith* to store her children. Or we may read, 'in order to store her children with (them).' 'Store' = provide.
721. pet of temperance, *i.e.* a sudden and transitory fit of temperance. pulse. So Daniel and his three companions refused the dainties of the King of Babylon and fed on pulse and water; *Dan.* i.
722. frieze, coarse woollen cloth.
723. All-giver. Comp. Gk. +pandôra+, an epithet applied to the earth as the giver of all.
725. 'And we should serve him as (if he were) a grudging master and a penurious niggard of his wealth, and (we should) live like Nature's bastards': see *Hebrews* xii. 8, "If ye are without chastening, whereof all have been made partakers, then are ye *bastards, and not sons.*"
728. Who. The pronoun here relates not to the word immediately preceding it, but to the substantive implied in the possessive pronoun *her*, *i.e.* the sons of her who. His, her, etc., in such constructions have their full force as genitives: comp. *L'Alleg.* 124, "her grace whom" = the grace of her whom. surcharged: overloaded, 'overfraught' (l. 732). waste fertility, wasted or unused abundance. This participial use of 'waste' seems to be due to the similarity in sound to such participles as 'elevate' (= elevated), 'instruct' (= instructed), etc., which occur in Milton (comp. *English Past and Present*, vi.).
729. strangled, suffocated.
730. winged air darked with plumes, *i.e.* the air being darkened by the flight of innumerable birds. Spenser also has *dark* as a verb. Both clauses in this line are absolute.
731. over-multitude, outnumber. This line and the preceding one illustrate the freedom with which, in earlier English, one part of speech was used for another.
732. o'erfraught: see note, l. 355.
733. emblaze, make to blaze, make splendid. There is perhaps a reference to the sense of *emblazon*, which is from M.E. *blazen*, to blaze abroad, to proclaim.
734. bestud with stars. In Milton's MS. it is 'bestud the centre with their star-light,' *centre* being the 'centre of the earth.'

735. inured, accustomed, by custom rendered less sensitive. *Inure* is from the old phrase 'in ure' = in operation (Fr. *oeuvre*, work).

737. coy: shy or reserved. cozened: cheated, beguiled. The origin of this word is interesting: a cozener is one who, for selfish ends, claims kindred or *cousinship* with another, and hence a flatterer or cheat.

739-755. Beauty is Nature's coin, etc. "The idea that runs through these seventeen lines is a favourite one with the old poets; and Warton and Todd cite parallel passages from Shakespeare, Daniel, Fletcher, and Drayton. Thus, from Shakespeare *(M. N. D.* i. 1. 76-8):

> "Earthlier happy is the rose distilled
> Than that which, withering on the virgin thorn,
> Grows, lives, and dies, in single blessedness."

See also Shakespeare's first six sonnets, which are pervaded by the idea in all its subtleties" (Masson).

743. let slip time, *i.e.* allow time *to* slip: see note, l. 304. Comp. *Par. Lost*, i. 178. "Let us not *slip* the occasion."

744. It = beauty. languished, languid or languishing: comp. *Par. Lost*, vi. 496, "their languished hope revived"; *Epitaph on M. of W.* 33. The suffix *-ed* is frequent in Elizabethan English where we now have *-ing* (Abbott, § 374).

747. most, as many as possible.

748. homely ... home. There is here a play upon words as in *Two Gent.* i. 1. 2: *"Home-keeping* youth have ever *homely* wits." *Homely* is derived from *home*.

749. Women with coarse complexions and dull cheeks are good enough for household occupations.

750. of sorry grain, not brilliant, of poor colour. 'Grain' is from Lat. *granum*, a seed, applied to small objects, and hence to the coccus or cochineal insect which yields a variety of red dyes. Hence *grain* came to denote certain colours, *e.g.* Tyrian purple, violet, etc., and is so used by Milton: see *Il Pens.* 33, "a robe of darkest *grain*"; *Par. Lost*, v. 285, "sky-tinctured *grain*"; xi. 242, "A military vest of purple ... Livelier than ... the *grain* Of Sarra," etc. And as these were fast or durable colours we have such phrases as 'to dye in grain,' 'a rogue in grain,' 'an

ingrained habit.' (See further in Marsh's *Lect. on Eng. Lang.* p. 55).

751. sampler, a sample or pattern piece of needlework. It is a doublet of *exemplar*. tease the huswife's wool. To *tease* is to comb or card: comp. the Lat. *vexare*. 'Huswife' = house-wife, further corrupted into *hussy*. *Hussif* (a case for needles, etc.) is a different word.

752. What need a vermeil-tinctured lip? See note, l. 362, on 'what need.' *Vermeil*: a French spelling of *vermilion*. The name is from Lat. *vermis*, a worm (the cochineal insect, from which the colour used to be got); and as *vermis* is cognate with Sansk. *krimi*, a worm, it follows that *vermilion*, *crimson*, and *carmine* are cognate.

753. tresses. Homer *(Odyssey*, v. 390) speaks of "the fair-tressed Dawn," +euplokamos Êôs+.

755. advised. Contrast with 'Advice,' l. 108.

756. Lines 756-761 are not addressed to Comus.

757. but that: were it not that.

758. as mine eyes: as he has already charmed mine eyes; see note, l. 170.

759. rules pranked in reason's garb, *i.e.* specious arguments. *Pranked* = decked in a showy manner: Milton (Prose works, i. 147, ed. 1698) speaks of the Episcopal church service *pranking* herself in the weeds of the Popish mass. Comp. *Wint. Tale*, iv. 4. 10, "Most goddess-like *prank'd* up"; *Par. Lost*, ii. 226, "Belial, with words clothed in *reason's garb*."

760-1. I hate when Vice brings forward refined arguments, and Virtue allows them to pass unchallenged. bolt = to sift or separate, as the *boulting-mill* separates the meal from the bran; in this sense the word (also spelt *boult*) is used by Chaucer, Spenser *(F. Q.* ii. 4. 24), Shakespeare *(Cor.* iii. 1. 322, *Wint. Tale*, iv. 4. 375, "the fanned snow that's *bolted* By the northern blasts twice o'er," etc.). The spelling *bolt* has confused the word with 'bolt,' to shoot or start out. See Index to Globe *Shakespeare*.

763. she would her children, etc., *i.e.* she wished (that) her children should be wantonly luxurious: comp. l. 172; *Par. Lost*, i. 497-503.

764. cateress, stewardess, provider: lit. 'a buyer.' *Cateress* is feminine: the masculine is *caterer*, where the final *-er* of the agent is unnecessarily repeated.

765. Means ... to the good: intends ... for the good.

767. dictate. The accent in Milton's time was on the first syllable, both in noun and verb. spare Temperance. For Milton's praises of Temperance comp. *Il Pens.* 46, "Spare Fast that oft with gods doth diet"; also the 6th Elegy, 56-66; *Son.* xx., etc. "There is much in the Lady which resembles the youthful Milton himself—he, the Lady of his college—and we may well believe that the great debate concerning temperance was not altogether dramatic (where, indeed, is Milton truly dramatic?), but was in part a record of passages in the poet's own spiritual history." Dowden's *Transcripts and Studies.*

768. If Nature's blessings were equally distributed instead of being heaped upon a luxurious few, then (as Shakespeare says, *King Lear*, iv. 1. 73) "distribution should undo excess, And each man have enough."

769. beseeming, suitable. The original sense of *seem* is 'to be fitting,' as in the words *beseem* and *seemly*.

770. lewdly-pampered; one of Milton's most expressive compounds = wickedly gluttonous. *Lewd* has passed through several changes of meaning: (1) the lay-people as distinct from the clergy; (2) ignorant or unlearned; and finally (2) base or licentious.

774. she no whit encumbered, *i.e.* Nature would not be in the least surcharged (as Comus represented in l. 728). *No whit*, used adverbially = not in the least, lit. 'not a particle.' Etymologically *aught* = a whit, *naught* = no whit.

776. His praise due paid, *i.e.* would be duly paid. On *due*, see note, l. 12. gluttony: abstract for concrete.

779. Crams, *i.e.* crams himself. There are many verbs in English that may be thus used reflexively without having the pronoun expressed, *e.g. feed, prepare, change, pour, press*, etc.

780. enow. 'Enow' conveys the notion of a number, as in early English: it is also spelt *anow*, and in Chaucer *ynowe*, and is the plural of *enough*. It still occurs as a provincialism in England. On lines 780-799 Masson says: "A recurrence, by the sister, with much more mystic fervour, to that Platonic and Miltonic

doctrine which had already been propounded by the Elder Brother (see lines 420-475)."

782. sun-clad power of chastity. With 'sun-clad' compare 'the sacred rays of chastity,' l. 425. Similarly in the *Faerie Queene*, iii. 6, Spenser says of Belphoebe, who represents Chastity, "And Phoebus with fair beams did her adorn."

783. yet to what end? A rhetorical question, = it would be to no purpose.

784. nor ... nor. These correlatives are often used in poetry for *neither* ... *nor* (Shakespeare often omitting the former altogether), and are equally correct. *Nor* is only a contraction of *neither*, and the first may as well be contracted as the second.

785. sublime notion and high mystery. In the *Apology for Smectymnuus* Milton tells of his study of the "divine volume of Plato," wherein he learned of the "abstracted sublimities" of Chastity and Love: also of his study of the Holy Scripture "unfolding these chaste and high mysteries, with timeless care infused, that the body is for the Lord, and the Lord for the body."

790. dear wit. 'Dear' is here used in contempt: its original sense is 'precious' (A.S. *deore*), but in Elizabethan English it has a variety of meanings, *e.g.* intense, serious, grievous, great, etc. Comp. "sad occasion *dear*," *Lyc.* 6; *"dear* groans," *L. L. L.* v. 2. 874. Craik suggests "that the notion properly involved in it of love, having first become generalised into that of a strong affection of any kind, had thence passed on to that of such an emotion the very reverse of love," as in my *dearest* foe. gay rhetoric: here so named in contempt, as being the instrument of sophistry.

791. fence, argumentation, *Fence* is an abbreviation of *defence*: comp. "tongue-fence" (Milton), "fencer in wits' school" (Fuller), *Much Ado*, v. 1. 75.

794. rapt spirits. 'Rapt' = enraptured, as if the mind or soul had been *carried out of itself* (Lat. *raptus*, seized): comp. *Il Pens.* 40, "Thy *rapt* soul sitting in thine eyes." Milton also uses the word of the actual snatching away of a person: "What accident hath *rapt* him from us," *Par. Lost*, ii. 40.

797. the brute Earth, etc., *i.e.* the senseless Earth would become sensible and assist me. 'Brute' = Lat. *brutus*, dull, insensible: comp. Horace, *Odes*, i. 34. 9, *"bruta tellus."*

800. She fables not: she speaks truly. This line is alliterative.

801. set off: comp. *Lyc.* 80, *"set off* to the world."

802. though not mortal: *sc.* 'I am.' shuddering dew. The epithet is, by hypallage, transferred from the person to the dew or cold sweat which 'dips' or moistens his body.

804. Speaks thunder and the chains of Erebus, etc.; in allusion to the *Titanomachia* or contest between Zeus and the Titans. Zeus, having been provided with thunder and lightning by the Cyclops, cast the Titans into Tartarus or Erebus, a region as far below Hell as Heaven is above the Earth. The leader of the Titans was Cronos (Saturn). There is a zeugma in *speaks* as applied to 'thunder' and 'chains,' unless it be taken as in both cases equivalent to *denounces*.

806. Come, no more! Comus now addresses the lady.

808. canon laws of our foundation, *i.e.* the established rules of our society. "A humorous application of the language of universities and other foundations" (Keightley).

809. 'tis but the lees, etc. *Lees* and *settlings* are synonymous = dregs. The allusion is to the old physiological system of the four primary humours of the body, viz. blood, phlegm, choler, and melancholy (see Burton's *Anat. of Mel.* i. 1, § ii. 2): "Melancholy, cold and dry, thick, black, and sour, begotten of the more feculent part of nourishment, and purged from the spleen"; Gk. +melancholia+, black bile. See *Sams. Agon.* 600, *"humours black* That mingle with thy fancy"; and Nash's *Terrors of the Night* (1594): "(Melancholy) sinketh down to the bottom like the lees of the wine, corrupteth the blood, and is the cause of lunacy."

811. straight, immediately. The adverb *straight* is now chiefly used of direction; to indicate time *straightway* (= in a straight way) is more usual: comp. *L'Alleg.* 69: "Straight mine eye hath caught new pleasures."

814. scape, a mutilated form of 'escape,' occurs both as a noun and a verb in Shakespeare and Milton: see *Par. Lost*, x. 5, "what can *scape* the eye of God?"; *Par. Reg.* ii. 189, "then lay'st thy *scapes* on names adored."

816. without his rod reversed. This use of the participle is a Latinism: see note, l. 48. At the same time it is to be noted that a phrase of this kind introduced by 'without' is in Latin

frequently rendered by the ablative absolute: such construction is here inadmissible because 'without' also governs 'mutters.'

817. backward mutters. The notion of a counter-charm produced by reversing the magical wand and by repeating the charm backwards occurs in Ovid *(Met.* xiv. 300), who describes Circe as thus restoring the followers of Ulysses to their human forms. Milton skilfully makes the neglect of the counter-charm the occasion for introducing the legend of Sabrina, which was likely to interest an audience assembled in the neighbourhood of the River Severn. On 'mutters,' see note, l. 526.

820. bethink me. The pronoun after this verb is reflexive. "The deliverance of their sister would be impossible but for supernatural interposition, the aid afforded by the Attendant Spirit from Jove's court. In other words, Divine Providence is asserted. Not without higher than human aid is the Lady rescued, and through the weakness of the mortal instruments of divine grace but half the intended work is accomplished." Dowden's *Transcripts and Studies.*

821. In this line and the next the attributive clauses are separated from the antecedent: see note, l. 2.

822. Meliboeus. The name of a shepherd in Virgil's *Eclogue* i. Possibly the poet Spenser is here meant, as the tale of Sabrina is given in the *Faerie Queene*, ii. 10, 14. The tale is also told by Geoffrey of Monmouth and by Sackville, Drayton and Warner. As Milton refers to a 'shepherd,' *i.e.* a poet, and to 'the soothest shepherd,' *i.e.* the truest poet, and as he follows Spenser's version of the story in this poem, we need not hesitate to identify Meliboeus with Spenser.

823. soothest, truest. The A.S. *sóth* meant *true*; hence also 'a true thing' = truth. It survives in *soothe* (lit. to affirm to be true), *soothsay* (see l. 874), and *forsooth* (= for a truth).

824. from hence. *Hence* represents an A.S. word *heonan*, *-an* being a suffix = from: so that in the phrase 'from hence' the force of the preposition is twice introduced. Yet the idiom is common: it arises from forgetfulness of the origin of the word. Comp. *Arc.* 3: "which *we from hence* descry."

825. with moist curb sways: comp. l. 18. Sabrina was a *numen fluminis* or river-deity.

826. Sabrina: The following is Milton's version of the legend:—
"After this, Brutus, in a chosen place, builds Troja Nova, changed in time to Trinovantum, now London; and began to enact laws (Heli being then High Priest in Judea); and, having governed the whole isle twenty-four years, died, and was buried in his new Troy. His three sons—Locrine, Albanact, and Camber—divide the land by consent. Locrine had the middle part, Loëgria; Camber possessed Cambria or Wales; Albanact, Albania, now Scotland. But he, in the end, by Humber, King of the Huns, who, with a fleet, invaded that land, was slain in fight, and his people driven back into Loëgria. Locrine and his brother go out against Humber; who now marching onward was by them defeated, and in a river drowned, which to this day retains his name. Among the spoils of his camp and navy were found certain young maids, and Estrilidis, above the rest, passing fair, the daughter of a king in Germany, from whence Humber, as he went wasting the sea-coast, had led her captive; whom Locrine, though before contracted to the daughter of Corineus, resolves to marry. But being forced and threatened by Corineus, whose authority and power he feared, Gwendolen the daughter he yields to marry, but in secret loves the other; and, ofttimes retiring as to some sacrifice, through vaults and passages made underground, and seven years thus enjoying her, had by her a daughter equally fair, whose name was Sabra. But when once his fear was off by the death of Corineus, not content with secret enjoyment, divorcing Gwendolen, he makes Estrilidis his Queen. Gwendolen, all in rage, departs into Cornwall; where Pladan, the son she had by Locrine, was hitherto brought up by Corineus, his grandfather; and gathering an army of her father's friends and subjects, gives battle to her husband by the river Sture, wherein Locrine, shot with an arrow, ends his life. But not so ends the fury of Gwendolen, for Estrilidis and her daughter Sabra she throws into a river, and, to have a monument of revenge, proclaims that the stream be thenceforth called after the damsel's name, which by length of time is changed now to *Sabrina* or Severn."—*History of Britain* (1670).

827. Whilom, of old. An obsolete word, lit. 'at time'; A.S. *hwílum*, instr. or dat. plur. of *hwíl*, time.

830. step-dame. For the actual relationship, see note, l. 826. The prefix *step* (A.S. *steóp-*) means 'orphaned,' and applies properly to a child whose parent has re-married: it was afterwards used in the words 'step-father,' etc. *Dame* (Fr. *dame*, a lady) retains the sense of mother in the form *dam*.

832. his = its: see note, l. 96.

834. pearled wrists, wrists adorned with pearls. An appropriate epithet, as pearls were said to exist in the waters of the Severn.

835. aged Nereus' hall, the abode of old Nereus, *i.e.* the bottom of the sea. Nereus, the father of the Nereids, or sea nymphs, is described as the wise and unerring old man of the sea; in Virgil, *grandaevus Nereus*. See also, l. 871, and compare Jonson's *Neptune's Triumph*, last song: "Old Nereus, with his fifty girls, From aged Indus laden home with pearls."

836. piteous of, *i.e.* full of pity for; comp. Lat. *miseret te aliorum* (genitive). Milton occasionally uses the word in this passive sense; its active sense is 'causing pity,' *i.e.* pitiful. Comp. Abbott, § 3. reared her lank head, *i.e.* raised up her drooping head: comp. *Par. Lost*, viii.: "In adoration at his feet I fell Submiss: he *reared* me." 'Lank,' lit. slender; hence weak. The adjective *lanky* is in common use = tall and thin.

837. imbathe, to bathe in: the force of the preposition being reduplicated, as in Lat. *incidere in*.

838. nectared lavers, etc., baths sweetened with nectar and scented with asphodel flowers. On 'nectar,' see note, l. 479. asphodel; the same, both name and thing, as 'daffodil' (see *Lyc.* 150, where it takes the form 'daffadillies'): Gk. +asphodelos+, M.E. *affodille*. The initial *d* in daffodil has not been satisfactorily explained: see l. 851.

839. the porch. So Quintilian calls the ear the vestibule of the mind: comp. *Haml.* i. 5. 63: "the porches of mine ear"; also the phrase, "the five gateways of knowledge."

840. ambrosial oils, oils of heavenly fragrance: see note, l. 16, and compare Virgil's use of *ambrosia* in *Georg.* iv. 415, *liquidum ambrosiae diffundit odorem*.

841. quick immortal change: comp. l. 10.

842. Made Goddess, etc. This participial construction is frequent in Milton as in Latin: it is equivalent to an explanatory clause.

844. twilight meadows: comp. "twilight groves," *Il Pens.* 133; "twilight ranks," *Arc.* 99; *Hymn Nat.* 188.

845. Helping all urchin blasts, remedying or preventing the blighting influence of evil spirits. 'Urchin blasts' is probably here used generally for what in *Arcades*, 49-53, are called "noisome winds and blasting vapours chill," 'urchin' being common in the sense of 'goblin' *(M. W. of W.* iv. 4. 49). Strictly the word denotes the hedgehog, which for various reasons was popularly regarded with great dread, and hence mischievous spirits were supposed to assume its form: comp. Shakespeare, *Temp*, i. 2. 326, ii. 2. 5, "Fright me with *urchin*-shows"; *Titus And.* ii. 3. 101; *Macbeth*, iv. 1. 2, "Thrice and once the *hedge-pig* whined," etc. Compare the protecting duties of the Genius in *Arcades*. Helping: comp. the phrases, "I cannot *help* it," *i.e.* prevent it; "it cannot be *helped*," *i.e.* remedied, etc.

846. shrewd. Here used in its radical sense = *shrew-ed*, malicious, like a shrew. Comp. *M. N. D.* ii. 1, "That *shrewd* and knavish sprite called Robin Goodfellow." Chaucer has the verb *shrew* = to curse; the current verb is *beshrew*.

847. vialed, contained in *phials*.

850. garland wreaths. A garland is a wreath, but we may take the phrase to mean 'wreathed garlands': comp. "twisted braids," l. 862.

852. old swain, *i.e.* Meliboeus (l. 862). "But neither Geoffrey of Monmouth nor Spenser has the development of the legend" (Masson).

853. clasping charm: see l. 613, 660.

854. warbled song: comp. *Arc.* 87, "touch the *warbled* string"; *Son.* xx. 12, *"Warble* immortal notes."

857. This will I try, *i.e.* to invoke her rightly in song.

858. adjuring, charging by something sacred and venerable. The adjuration is contained in lines 867-889, which, in Milton's MS., are directed "to be said," not sung, and in the Bridgewater MS. "to sing or not." From the latter MS. it would appear that these lines were sung as a kind of trio by Lawes and the two brothers.

863. amber-dropping: see note, l. 333; and comp. l. 106, where the idea is similar, warranting us in taking 'amber-dropping' as a compound epithet = dropping amber, and not (as some read)

'amber' and 'dropping.' *Amber* conveys the ideas of luminous clearness and fragrance: see *Sams. Agon*. 720, *"amber* scent of odorous perfume."

865. silver lake, the Severn. Virgil has the Lat. *lacus* in the sense of 'a river.'

868. great Oceanus, Gk. +Ôkeanon te megan+. The early Greeks regarded the earth as a flat disc, surrounded by a perpetually flowing river called Oceanus: the god of this river was also called Oceanus, and afterwards the name was applied to the Atlantic. Hesiod, Drayton, and Jonson have all applied the epithet 'great' to the god Oceanus; in fact, throughout these lines Milton uses what may be called the "permanent epithets" of the various divinities.

869. earth-shaking Neptune's mace, *i.e.* the trident of Poseidon (Neptune). Homer calls him +ennosigaios+ = earth-shaking: comp. *Iliad*, xii. 27, "And the Shaker of the Earth with his trident in his hands," etc. In *Par. Lost*, x. 294, Milton provides Death with a "mace petrifick."

870. Tethys' . . . pace. Tethys, wife of Oceanus, their children being the Oceanides and river-gods. In Hesiod she is 'the venerable' (+potnia Têthys+), and in Ovid 'the hoary.'

871. hoary Nereus: see note, l. 835.

872. Carpathian wizard's hook. See Virgil's *Georg*. iv. 387, "In the sea-god's Carpathian gulf there lives a seer, Proteus, of the sea's own hue . . . all things are known to him, those which are, those which have been, and those which drag their length through the advancing future." *Wizard* = diviner, without the depreciatory sense of line 571; see note there. *Hook*: Proteus had a shepherd's hook, because he tended "the monstrous herds of loathly sea-calves": *Odyssey*, iv. 385-463.

873. scaly Triton's . . . shell. In *Lycidas*, 89, he is "the Herald of the Sea." He bore a 'wreathed horn' or shell which he blew at the command of Neptune in order to still the restless waves of the sea. He was 'scaly,' the lower part of his body being like that of a fish.

874. soothsaying Glaucus. He was a Boeotian fisherman who had been changed into a marine deity, and was regarded by fishermen and sailors as a soothsayer or oracle: see note, l. 823.

875. Leucothea: lit. "the white goddess" (Gk. +leukê+, +thea+), the name by which Ino, the daughter of Cadmus, was worshipped after she had thrown herself into the sea to avoid her enraged husband Athamas.

876. her son, *i.e.* Melisertes, drowned and deified along with his mother: as a sea-deity he was called Palaemon, identified by the Romans with their god of harbours, Portumnus.

877. tinsel-slippered. The 'permanent epithet' of Thetis, a daughter of Nereus and mother of Achilles, is "silver-footed" (Gk. +argyropeza+). Comp. *Neptune's Triumph* (Jonson):

"And all the silver-footed nymphs were drest
To wait upon him, to the Ocean's feast."

'Tinsel-slippered' is a paraphrase of this, for 'tinsel' is a cloth worked with silver (or gold): the notion of cheap finery is not radical. Etymologically, *tinsel* is that which glitters or *scintillates*. On the beauty of this epithet, and of Milton's compound epithets generally, see Trench, *English Past and Present*, p. 296.

878-80. Sirens ... Parthenopè's ... Ligea's. The three Sirens (see note, l. 253) were Parthenopè, Lig{=e}a, and Lucosia. The tomb of the first was at Naples (see Milton's *Ad Leonaram*, iii., "Credula quid liquidam Sirena, Neapoli, jactas, Claraque Parthenopes fana Achelöiados," etc.). Ligea, described by Virgil *(Georg.* iv. 336) as a sea-nymph, is here represented as seated, like a mermaid, in the act of smoothing her hair with a golden comb.

881. Wherewith = with which. The true adjective clause is "sleeking ... locks" = with which she sleeks, etc.; and the true participial clause is "she sits ... rocks" = seated on ... rocks.

882. Sleeking, making sleek or glossy. The original sense of 'sleek' is greasy: comp. *Lyc.* 99, "On the level brine *Sleek* Panopè with all her sisters played."

885. heave, raise. Comp. the similar use of the word in *L'Alleg.* 145, "Orpheus' self may heave his head."

887. bridle in, *i.e.* restrain.

888. have: subjunctive after *till*, as frequently in Milton.

890. rushy-fringèd, fringed with rushes. The more usual form would be rush-fringed: we may regard Milton's form as a participle formed from the compound noun "rushy-fringe": comp. 'blue-haired,' l. 29; "false-played," Shakespeare, *A. and C.* iv. 14.

891. grows. A singular with two nominatives connected by *and*: the verb is to be taken with each. But the compound subject is really equivalent to "the willow with its osiers dank," osiers being water-willows or their branches. dank, damp: comp. *Par. Lost*, vii. 441, "oft they quit the *dank*" (= the water).

893. Thick set, etc., *i.e.* thickly inlaid with agate and beautified with the azure sheen of turquoise, etc. There is a zeugma in *set.* azurn sheen. Sheen = brightness: it occurs again in l. 1003; see note there. 'Azurn': modern English has a tendency to use the noun itself as an adjective in cases where older English used an adjective with the suffix *-en* = made of. Most of the adjectives in *-en* that still survive do not now denote "made of," but simply "like," *e.g.* golden hair, etc. *Azurn* and *cedarn* (l. 990), *hornen*, *treen*, *corden*, *glassen*, *reeden*, etc., are practically obsolete; see Trench, *English Past and Present.* Comp. 'oaten' *(Lyc.* 33), 'oaken' *(Arc.* 45). As the words 'azurn' and 'cedarn' are peculiar to Milton some hold that he adopted them from the Italian *azzurino* and *cedrino*.

894. turkis; also spelt turkoise, turquois, and turquoise: lit. 'the Turkish stone,' a Persian gem so called because it came through Turkey (Pers. *turk*, a Turk).

895. That . . . strays. Milton does not imply that these stones were found in the Severn, nor does he in lines 932-937 imply that cinnamon grows on its banks.

897. printless feet. Comp. *Temp.* v. i. 34: "Ye that on the sands with *printless foot* Do chase the ebbing Neptune"; also *Arc.* 85: "Where no print of step hath been."

902. It will be noticed that the Spirit takes up the rhymes of Sabrina's song ('here,' 'dear'; 'request,' 'distressed'), and again Sabrina continues the rhymes of the Spirit's song ('distressed,' 'best').

913. of precious cure, of curative power. See note on this use of 'of,' l. 155.

914. References to the efficacy of sprinkling are frequent, *e.g.* in the English Bible, in Spenser, in Virgil *(Aen.* vi. 229), in Ovid *(Met.* iv. 479), in *Par. Lost*, xi. 416.

916. Next: an adverb modifying 'touch.'

917. glutinous, sticky, viscous. The epithet is transferred from the effect to the cause.

921. Amphitrite: the wife of Neptune (Poseidon) and goddess of the Sea.

923. Anchises line: see note, l. 827. Locrine was the son of Brutus, who was the son of Silvius, who was the grandson of the great Aeneas, who was the son of old Anchises.

924. may ... miss. This verb is optative: so are '(may) scorch,' '(may) fill,' 'may roll,' and 'may be crowned.'

925. brimmèd. The passive participle is so often used where we now use the active that 'brimmed' may mean 'brimming' = full to the brim. On the other hand, 'brim' is frequent in the sense of *bank* (comp. l. 119), so that some regard 'brimmed' as = enclosed within banks.

928. singèd, scorched. We should rather say 'scorching.' On the good wishes expressed in lines 924-937 Masson's comment is: "The whole of this poetic blessing on the Severn and its neighbourhood, involving the wish of what we should call 'solid commercial prosperity,' would go to the heart of the assemblage at Ludlow."

933. beryl: in the Bible *(Rev.* xxi. 20) this precious stone forms one of the foundations of the New Jerusalem. The word is of Eastern origin: comp. Arab, *billaur*, crystal. golden ore. As a matter of fact gold has been found in the Welsh mountains.

934. May thy lofty head, etc. The grammatical construction is: 'May thy lofty head be crowned round with many a tower and terrace, and here and there (may thy lofty head be crowned) with groves of myrrh and cinnamon (growing) upon thy banks.' This makes 'banks' objective, and 'upon' a preposition: the only objection to this reading is that the notion of crowning the head upon the banks is peculiar. The difficulty vanishes when we recollect that Milton frequently connects two clauses with one subject rather loosely: the subject of the second clause is 'thou,' implied in 'thy lofty head.' An exact parallel to this is found in *L'Alleg.* 121, 122:

'whose bright eyes rain influence and *judge* the prize'; also in *Il Pens*. 155-7; 'let my due feet never fail to *walk . . . and love*, etc.': also in *Lyc*. 88, 89. The explanation adopted by Prof. Masson is that Milton had in view two Greek verbs—+peristephanoô+, 'to put a crown round,' and +epistephanoô+, "to put a crown upon": thus, "May thy lofty head be *crowned round* with many a tower and terrace, and thy banks here and there be *crowned upon* with groves of myrrh and cinnamon." This makes 'banks' nominative, and 'upon' an adverb.

In the Bridgewater MS. the stage direction here is, *Song ends*.

942. Not a waste, etc., *i.e.* 'Let there not be a superfluous or unnecessary sound until we come.' 'waste' is an attributive: see note, l. 728.

945. gloomy covert wide: see note, l. 207.

946. not many furlongs. These words are deliberately inserted to keep up the illusion. It is probable that, in the actual representation of the mask, the scene representing the enchanted palace was removed when Comus's rout was driven off the stage, and a woodland scene redisplayed. This would give additional significance to these lines and to the change of scene after l. 957. 'Furlong' = furrow-long: it thus came to mean the length of a field, and is now a measure of length.

949. many a friend. 'Many a' is a peculiar idiom, which has been explained in different ways. One view is that 'many' is a corruption of the French *mesnie*, a train or company, and 'a' a corruption of the preposition 'of,' the singular noun being then substituted for the plural through confusion of the preposition with the article. A more correct view seems to be that 'many' is the A.S. *manig*, which was in old English used with a singular noun and without the article, *e.g. manig mann* = many men. In the thirteenth century the indefinite article began to be inserted; thus *mony enne thing* = many a thing, just as we say 'what *a* thing,' 'such *a* thing.' This would seem to show that 'a' is not a corruption of 'of,' and that there is no connection with the French word *mesnie*. Milton, in this passage, uses 'many a friend' with a plural verb. gratulate. The simple verb is now replaced by the compound *congratulate* (Lat. *gratulari*, to wish joy to a person).

950. wished, *i.e.* wished for; see note, l. 574. and beside, *i.e.* 'and where, besides,' etc.

952. jigs, lively dances.

958. Back, shepherds, back! On the rising of the curtain, the stage is occupied by peasants engaged in a merry dance. Soon after the attendant Spirit enters with the above words. Enough your play, *i.e.* we have had enough of your dancing, which must now give way to 'other trippings.'

959. sunshine holiday. Comp. *L'Alleg.* 98, where the same expression is used. There is a close resemblance between the language of this song and lines 91-99 of *L'Allegro*. Milton's own spelling of 'holiday' is 'holyday,' which shows the origin of the word. The accent in such compounds (comp. blue-bell, blackbird, etc.) falls on the adjective: it is only in this way that the ear can tell whether the compound forms *(e.g.* hóliday) or the separate words *(e.g.* hóly dáy) are being used.

960. Here be: see note, l. 12. without duck or nod: words used to describe the ungraceful dancing and awkward courtesy of the country people.

961. trippings ... lighter toes ... court guise: words used to describe the graceful movements of the Lady and her brothers: comp. *L'Alleg.* 33: "trip it, as you go, On the light fantastic toe." *Trod* (or trodden), past participle of *tread*: 'to tread a measure' is a common expression, meaning 'to dance.' 'Court guise,' *i.e.* courtly mien; *guise* is a doublet of *wise* = way, *e.g.* 'in this wise,' 'like*wise*,' 'other*wise*.' In such pairs of words as *guise* and *wise*, *guard* and *ward*, *guile* and *wile*, the forms in *gu* have come into English through the French.

963. Mercury (the Greek Hermes) was the herald of the gods, and as such was represented as having winged ankles (Gk. +ptênopedilos+): his name is here used as a synonym both for agility and refinement.

964. mincing Dryades. The Dryades are wood-nymphs (Gk. +drys+, a tree), here represented as mincing, *i.e.* tripping with short steps, unlike the clumsy striding of the country people. Comp. *Merch. of V.* iii. 4. 67: "turn two *mincing* steps Into a manly stride." Applied to a person's gait (or speech), the word now implies affectation.

965. lawns ... leas. On 'lawn,' see note, l. 568: a 'lea' is a meadow.
966. This song is sung by Lawes while presenting the three young persons to the Earl and Countess of Bridgewater.
967. ye: see note, l. 216.
968. so goodly grown, *i.e.* grown so goodly. *Goodly* = handsome (A.S. *gódlic* = goodlike).
970. timely. Here an adverb: in l. 689 it is an adjective. Comp. the two phrases in *Macbeth*: "To gain the *timely* inn," iii. 3. 7; and "To call *timely* on him," ii. 3. 51.
972. assays, trials, temptations. *Assay* is used by Milton in the sense of 'attempt' as well as of 'trial': see *Arc.* 80, "I will *assay*, her worth to celebrate." The former meaning is now confined to the form *essay* (radically the same word); and the use of *assay* has been still further restricted from its being used chiefly of the testing of metals. Comp. *Par. Lost*, iv. 932, "hard *assays* and ill successes"; *Par. Reg.* i. 264, iv. 478.
974, 5. To triumph. The whole purpose of the poem is succinctly expressed in these lines. *Stage Direction*: Spirit epiloguizes, *i.e.* sings the epilogue or concluding stanzas. In one of Lawes' manuscripts of the mask, the epilogue consists of twelve lines only, those numbered 1012-1023. From the same copy we find that line 976 had been altered by Lawes in such a manner as to convert the first part of the epilogue into a prologue which, in his character as Attendant Spirit, he sang whilst descending upon the stage:—

> *From the heavens* now I fly,
> And those happy climes that lie
> Where day never shuts his eye,
> Up in the broad *field* of the sky.
> There I suck the liquid air
> All amidst the gardens fair
> Of Hesperus, and his daughters three
> That sing about the golden tree.
> There eternal summer dwells,
> And west winds, with musky wing,
> About the cedarn alleys fling
> Nard and cassia's balmy smells.
> Iris there with humid bow

>Waters the odorous banks, that blow
>Flowers of more mingled hue
>Than her purfled scarf can show,
>*Yellow, watchet, green, and blue,*
>And drenches oft with *Manna* dew
>Beds of hyacinth and roses,
>Where *many a cherub soft* reposes.

    Doubtless this was the arrangement in the actual performance of the mask.

976. To the ocean, etc. The resemblance of this song, in rhythm and rhyme, to the song of Ariel in the *Tempest*, v. 1. 88-94, has been frequently pointed out: "Where the bee sucks, there suck I," etc. Compare also the song of Johphiel in *The Fortunate Isles* (Ben Jonson): "Like a lightning from the sky," etc. The epilogue as sung by Lawes (ll. 1012-1023) may also be compared with the epilogue of the *Tempest*: "Now my charms are all o'erthrown," etc.

977. happy climes. Comp. *Odyssey*, iv. 566: "The deathless gods will convey thee to the Elysian plain and the world's end ... where life is easiest for men. No snow is there, nor yet great storm, nor any rain; but always ocean sendeth forth the breeze of the shrill west to blow cool on men": see also l. 14. 'Clime,' radically the same as *climate*, is still used in its literal sense = a region of the earth; while 'climate' has the secondary meaning of 'atmospheric conditions.' Comp. *Son.* viii. 8: "Whatever *clime* the sun's bright circle warms."

978. day ... eye. Comp. *Son.* i. 5: "the *eye* of day"; and *Lyc.* 26: "the opening *eyelids* of the Morn."

979. broad fields of the sky. Comp. Virgil's *"Aëris in campis latis,"* *Aen.* vi. 888.

980. suck the liquid air, inhale the pure air. 'Liquid' (lit. flowing) is used figuratively and generally in the sense of pure and sweet: comp. *Son.* i. 5, "thy liquid notes."

981. All amidst. For this adverbial use of *all* (here modifying the following prepositional phrase), compare *Il Pens.* 33, *"all* in a robe of darkest grain."

982. Hesperus: see note, l. 393. Hesperus, the brother of Atlas, had three daughters—Aegle, Cynthia, and Hesperia. They were

famed for their sweet song. In Milton's MS. *Hesperus* is written over *Atlas*: Spenser makes them daughters of Atlas, as does Jonson in *Pleasure reconciled to Virtue*.

984. crispéd shades. 'Crisped,' like 'curled' (comp. "curl the grove," *Arc.* 46) is a common expression in the poetry of the time, and has the same meaning. The original form is the adjective 'crisp' (Lat. *crispus* = curled), from which comes the verb *to crisp* and the participle *crisped*. Compare "the *crisped* brooks . . . ran nectar," *Par. Lost*, iv. 237, where the word is best rendered 'rippled'; also Tennyson's *Claribel*, 19, "the babbling runnel *crispeth*." In the present case the reference is to the foliage of the trees.

985. spruce, gay. This word, now applied to persons with a touch of levity, was formerly used both of things and persons in the sense of gay or neat. Compare the present and earlier uses of the word *jolly*, on which Pattison says:—"This is an instance of the disadvantage under which poetry in a living language labours. No knowledge of the meaning which a word bore in 1631 can wholly banish the later and vulgar associations which may have gathered round it since. Apart from direct parody and burlesque, the tendency of living speech is gradually to degrade the noble; so that as time goes on the range of poetical expression grows from generation to generation more and more restricted." The origin of the word *spruce* is disputed: Skeat holds that it is a corruption of Pruce (old Fr. *Pruce*, mod. Fr. *Prusse*) = Prussia; we read in the 14th century of persons dressed after the fashion of Prussia or Spruce, and Prussia was called Sprussia by some English writers up to the beginning of the 17th century. See also Trench, *Select Glossary*.

986. The Graces. The three Graces of classical mythology were Euphrosyne (the light-hearted one), Aglaia (the bright one), and Thalia (the blooming one). See *L'Alleg.* 12: "Euphrosyne . . . Whom lovely Venus, at a birth, With two sister Graces more, To ivy-crownèd Bacchus bore." They were sometimes represented as daughters of Zeus, and as the goddesses who purified and enhanced all the innocent pleasures of life. rosy-bosomed Hours. The Hours (Horæ) of classical mythology were the goddesses of the Seasons, whose course was described as the dance of the Horæ. The Hora of Spring accompanied

Persephone every year on her ascent from the lower world, and the expression "The chamber of the Horæ opens" is equivalent to "The Spring is coming." 'Rosy-bosomed'; the Gk. +rhodokolpos+: compare the epithets 'rosy-fingered' (applied by Homer to the dawn), 'rosy-armed,' etc.

989. musky ... fling. Compare *Par. Lost*, viii. 515: "Fresh gales and gentle airs Whispered it to the woods, and from their wings Flung rose, flung odours from the spicy shrub." In this passage the verb *fling* is similarly used. 'Musky' = fragrant: comp. 'musk-rose,' l. 496.

990. cedarn alleys, *i.e.* alleys of cedar trees. For 'alley,' comp. l. 311. For the form of 'cedarn,' see note on 'azurn,' l. 893. Tennyson uses the word 'cedarn' in *Recoll. of Arab. Nights*, 115.

991. Nard and cassia; two aromatic plants. Cassia is a name sometimes applied to the wild cinnamon: nard is also called *spike-nard*; see allusion in the Bible, *Mark*, xiv. 3; *Exod.* xxx. 24, etc.

992. Iris ... humid bow: see note, l. 83. The allusion is, of course, to the rainbow.

993. blow, here used actively = cause to blossom: comp. Jonson, *Mask at Highgate*, "For thee, Favonius, here shall *blow* New flowers."

995. purfled = having an embroidered edge (O.F. *pourfiler*): the verb *to purfle* survives in the contracted form *to purl*, and is cognate with profile = a front line or edge. shew: here rhymes with *dew*; comp. l. 511, 512. This points to the fact that in Milton's time the present pronunciation of *shew*, though familiar, was not the only one recognised.

996. drenches with Elysian dew, *i.e.* soaks with heavenly dew. The Homeric Elysium is described in *Odyssey*, iv.: see note, l. 977; it was afterwards identified with the abode of the blessed, l. 257. *Drench* is the causative of *drink*: here the nominative of the verb is 'Iris' and the object 'beds.'

997. if your ears be true, *i.e.* if your ears be pure: the poet is about to speak of that which cannot be understood by those with "gross unpurgèd ear" *(Arc.* 73, and *Com.* l. 458). He alludes to that pure Love which "leads up to Heaven," *Par. Lost*, viii. 612.

998. hyacinth. This is the "sanguine flower inscribed with woe" of *Lycidas*, 106: it sprang from the blood of Hyacinthus, a youth beloved by Apollo.

999. Adonis, the beloved of Venus, died of a wound which he received from a boar during the chase. The grief of Venus was so great that the gods of the lower world allowed him to spend six months of every year on earth. The story is of Asiatic origin, and is supposed to be symbolic of the revival of nature in spring and its death in winter. Comp. *Par. Lost*, ix. 439, "those gardens feigned Or of revived Adonis," etc.

1000. waxing well of, *i.e.* recovering from. The A.S. *weaxan* = to grow or increase: Shakespeare has 'man of wax' = adult, *Rom. and Jul.* i. 3. 76; see also Index to Globe *Shakespeare*.

1002. Assyrian queen, *i.e.* Venus, whose worship came from the East, probably from Assyria. She was originally identical with Astarte, called by the Hebrews Ashteroth: see *Par. Lost*, i. 438-452, where Adonis appears as Thammuz.

1003, 4. far above ... advanced. These words are to be read together: 'advanced' is an attribute to 'Cupid,' and is modified by 'far above.'

1003. spangled sheen, glittering brightness. 'Spangled': *spangle* is a diminutive of *spang* = a metal clasp, and hence 'a shining ornament.' In poetry it is common to speak of the stars as 'spangles' and of the heavens as 'spangled': comp. Addison's well-known lines:

> "The spacious firmament on high,
> With all the blue ethereal sky,
> And *spangled* heavens, a shining frame,
> Their great Original proclaim."

Comp. also *Lyc.* 170, "with *new-spangled* ore." 'Sheen' is here used as a noun, as in line 893; also in *Hymn Nat.* 145, "throned in celestial *sheen*": *Epitaph on M. of W.* 73, "clad in radiant *sheen*." The word occurs in Spenser as an adjective also: comp. "her dainty corse so fair and *sheen*," *F. Q.* ii. 1. 10. In the line "By fountain clear or spangled starlight *sheen*" *(M. N. D.* ii. l. 29) it is doubtful whether the word is a noun or an

139

adjective. Milton uses the adjective *sheeny (Death of Fair Infant,* 48).

1004. Celestial Cupid. The ordinary view of Cupid is given in the note to line 445; here he is the lover of Psyche (the human soul) to whom he is united after she has been purified by a life of trial and misfortune. The myth of Cupid and Psyche is as follows: Cupid was in love with Psyche, but warned her that she must not seek to know who he was. Yielding to curiosity, however, she drew near to him with a lamp while he was asleep. A drop of the hot oil falling on him, he awoke, and fled from her. She now wandered from place to place, persecuted by Venus; but after great sorrow, during which she was secretly supported by Cupid, she became immortal and was united to him for ever. In this story Psyche represents the human soul (Gk. +psychê+), which is disciplined and purified by earthly misfortune and so fitted for the enjoyment of true happiness in heaven. Further, in Milton's Allegory it is only the soul so purified that is capable of knowing true love: in his *Apology for Smectymnuus* he calls it that Love "whose charming cup is only virtue," and whose "first and chiefest office ... begins and ends in the soul, producing those happy twins of her divine generation, Knowledge and Virtue." To this high and mystical love Milton again alludes in *Epitaphium Damonis*:

> "In other part, the expansive vault above,
> And there too, even there the god of love;
> With quiver armed he mounts, his torch displays
> A vivid light, his gem-tipt arrows blaze,
> Around his bright and fiery eyes he rolls,
> Nor aims at vulgar minds or little souls,
> Nor deigns one look below, but aiming high
> Sends every arrow to the lofty sky;
> Hence forms divine, and minds immortal, learn
> The power of Cupid, and enamoured burn."
> *Cowper's translation.*

1007. among: preposition governing 'gods.'
1008. make: subjunctive after 'till.' Its nominative is 'consent.'

1010. blissful, blest. *Bliss* is cognate with *bless* and *blithe*. Comp. "the *blest* kingdoms meek of joy and love," *Lyc.* 177. are to be born. There seems to be here a confusion of constructions between the subjunctive co-ordinate with *make* and the indicative dependent in meaning on "Jove hath sworn" in the following line.

1011. Youth and Joy. Everlasting youth and joy are found only after the trials of earth are past. So Spenser makes Pleasure the daughter of Cupid and Psyche, but she is "the daughter late," *i.e.* she is possible only to the purified soul. See also note on l. 1004.

1012. my task, *i.e.* the task alluded to in line 18. This line is an adverbial clause = Now that (or *because*) my task is smoothly done.

1013. The Spirit's task being finished he is free to soar where he pleases. There seems to be implied the injunction that mankind can by virtue alone attain to the same spiritual freedom.

1014. green earth's end. The world as known to the ancients did not extend much beyond the Straits of Gibraltar. The Cape Verd Islands, which lie outside these straits, may be here referred to: comp. *Par. Lost*, viii. 630:

> "But I can now no more; the parting sun
> Beyond the earth's green Cape and Verdant Isles
> Hesperean sets, my signal to depart."

1015. bowed welkin: the meaning of the line is, "Where the arched sky curves slowly towards the horizon." *Welkin* is, radically, "the region of clouds," A.S. *wolcnu*, clouds.

1017. corners of the moon, *i.e.* its horns. The crescent moon is said to be 'horned' (Lat. *cornu*, a horn). Comp. the lines in *Macbeth*, iii. 5. 23, 24: "Upon the corners of the moon There hangs a vaporous drop profound."

1020. She can teach ye how to climb, etc. Compare Jonson's song to Virtue:

> "Though a stranger here on earth
> In heaven she hath her right of birth.
> There, there is Virtue's seat:
> Strive to keep her your own;

>'Tis only she can make you great,
>Though place here make you known."

1021. sphery chime, *i.e.* the music of the spheres. "To climb higher than the sphery chime" means to ascend beyond the spheres into the empyrean or true heaven—the abode of God and the purest Spirits. Milton therefore implies that by virtue alone can we come into God's presence. See note on "the starry quire," line 112. 'Chime' is strictly 'harmony,' as in "silver *chime*," *Hymn Nat.* 128: the word is cognate with *cymbal*.

1022, 3. if Virtue feeble were, etc. A triumphant expression of that confidence in the invincibleness of virtue, when aided by Divine Providence, and therefore a fitting conclusion of the whole masque. Milton's whole life reveals his unshaken belief in the truth expressed in the last two lines of his *Comus*.

INDEX TO THE NOTES.

A.

Acheron, 604.
Adonis, 999.
Adventurous, 79.
Advice, 108;
　advised, 755.
Affects, 386.
Alabaster, 660.
All, 714, 981.
All ear, 560.
Alley, 311, 990.
All-giver, 723.
All to-ruffled, 380.
Amber-dropping, 863.
Ambrosial, 16.
Amiss, 177.
Apace, 657.
Arbitrate, 411.
Asphodel, 838.
Assays, 972.
Assyrian Queen, 1002.
Ay me, 511.
Azurn, 893.

B.

Backward, 817.
Baited, 162.

Bandite, 426.
Be, 12, 519.
Benison, 332.
Beryl, 933.
Beseeming, 769.
Blank, 452.
Blissful, 1010.
Blue-haired, 29.
Blow, 993.
Bolt, 760.
Bosky, 313.
Bourn, 313.
Brakes, 147.
Brimmed, 925.
Brinded, 443.
Brute, 797.
Budge, 707.
Burs, 352.

C.

Cassia, 991.
Cast, 360.
Cateress, 764.
Cedarn, 990.
Centre, 382.
Certain, 266.
Chance, 508.
Charactered, 530.
Charmèd, 51.
Charnel, carnal, 471.
Charybdis, 257.
Chime, 1021.
Chimeras, 517.
Circe, 50.
Clime, 977.
Close, 548.
Clouted, 635.
Company, 274.

Comus, 46, 58.
Convoy, 81.
Cordial, 672.
Corners, 1017.
Cotes, 344.
Cotytto, 129.
Courtesy, 325.
Cozened, 737.
Crabbed, 477.
Crisped, 984.
Crofts, 531.
Crowned, 934.
Curfew, 435.
Curious, 714.
Cynic, 708.
Cynosure, 342.

D.

Dapper, 118.
Darked, 730.
Dear, 790.
Dell, 312.
Descry, 141.
Dew-besprent, 542.
Dimple, 119.
Dingle, 312.
Disinherit, 334.
Ditty, 86.
Drench, 996.
Drouth, 66.
Drowsy frighted, 553.
Due, 12.
Dun, 127.
Durst, 577.

E.

Each ... every, 19, 311.
Earth-shaking, 869.
Ebon, 134.
Ecstasy, 261, 625.
Element, 299.
Elysium, 257.
Emblaze, 732.
Emprise, 610.
Engaged, 193.
Enow, 780.
Erebus, 804.
Every ... each, 19, 311.
Eye, 329.

F.

Faery, 298.
Fairly, 168.
Fantastic, 144, 205.
Fence, 791.
Firmament, 598.
Fond, 67.
For, 586, 602.
Forestalling, 285.
Forlorn, 39.
Fraught, 355, 732.
Freezed, 449.
Frighted, 553.
Frolic, 59.

G.

Gear, 167.
Glistering, 219.
Glozing, 161.
Goodly, 968.
Graces, 986.
Grain, 750.

Granges, 175.
Gratulate, 949.
Grisly, 603.
Guise, 961.

H.

Haemony, 638.
Hag, 434.
Hallo, 226.
Hapless, 350.
Harpies, 605.
Harrowed, 565.
Heave, 885.
Hecate, 135.
Help, 304, 845.
Hence, 824.
Her, 351, 455.
Hesperian, 393.
High, 654.
Hinds, 174.
Holiday, 959.
Home-felt, 262.
Homely, 748.
Horror, 38.
Hours, 986.
How chance, 508.
Huswife, 751.
Hutched, 719.
Hyacinth, 998.
Hydras. 605.

I.

Imbathe, 837.
Imbodies, 468.
Imbrutes, 468.
Immured, 521.
Infamous, 424.

Infer, 408.
Influence, 336.
Inlay, 22.
Innumerous, 349.
Insphered, 3.
Interwove, 544.
Inured, 735.
Iris, 83.
Isle, 21.

J.

Jocund, 172.
Jollity, 104.
Julep, 672.

K.

Knot-grass, 542.

L.

Lackey, 455.
Lake, 865.
Languished, 744.
Lank, 836.
Lap, 257.
Lawn, 568.
Lees, 809.
Leucothea, 875.
Lewdly-pampered, 770.
Like, 22, 634.
Lime-twigs, 646.
Liquid, 980.
Liquorish, 700.
Listed, 49.
Listened, 551.
Liveried, 455.
Lore, 34.

Love-lorn, 234.
Luscious, 652.

M.

Madness, 261.
Madrigal, 495.
Mansion, 2.
Mantling, 294.
Many a, 949.
Margent, 232.
Me, 163, 630.
Meander, 232.
Meditate, 547.
Melancholy, 810.
Methought, 171.
Meliboeus, 822.
Mickle, 31.
Mildew, 640.
Mincing, 964.
Mintage, 529.
Misusèd, 47.
Moly, 636.
Monstrous, 533.
Mountaineer, 426.
Morrice, 116.
Mortal, 10.
Murmurs, 526.
Mutters, 817.
My, mine, 170.

N.

Naiades, 254.
Nard, 991.
Navel, 520.
Necromancer, 649.
Nectar, 479.
Neighbour, 484.

Nepenthes, 675.
Nereus, 835.
Nether, 20.
New-intrusted, 36.
Nice, 139.
Night-foundered, 483.
Nightingale, 234.
Nightly, 113.
Nor . . . nor, 784.

O.

Oaten, 345, 893.
Oceanus, 97, 868.
Of, 59, 155, 836, 1000.
Ominous, 61.
Orient, 65.
Other, 612.
Oughly-headed, 695.
Ounce, 71.
Over-exquisite, 359.
Over-multitude, 731.

P.

Palmer, 189.
Pan, 176.
Pard, 444.
Parley, 241.
Pent, 499.
Perfect, 73, 203.
Perplexed, 37.
Pert, 118.
Pestered, 7.
Pinfold, 7.
Plight, 372.
Plighted, 301
Plumes, 378.
Potion, 68.

Pranked, 759.
Presentments, 156.
Prime, 289.
Prithee, 615.
Prove, 123.
Purchase, 607.
Purfled, 995.
Psyche, 1004.

Q.

Quaint, 157.
Quarters, 29.
Quire, 112.
Quivered, 422.

R.

Rapt, 794.
Ravishment, 244.
Reared, 836.
Recks, 404.
Regard, 620.
Rifted, 518.
Rite, 125.
Roost, 317.
Rosy-bosomed, 986.
Rout, 92-93.
Rule, 340.
Rushy-fringed, 890.

S.

Sabrina, 826.
Sadly, 509.
Sampler, 751.
Saws, 110.
Scape, 814.
Scylla, 257.

Serene, 4.
Several, 25.
Shagged, 429.
Shapes, 2.
Sheen, 893, 1003.
Shell, 231, 837.
Shew, 995.
Shoon, 635.
Should, 482.
Shrewd, 846.
Shrouds, 147.
Shuddering, 802.
Siding, 212.
Simples, 627.
Single, 204.
Sirens, 253, 878.
Sleeking, 882.
Slope, 98.
Solemnity, 142.
Soothest, 823.
Sooth-saying, 874.
Sounds, 115.
Sovran, 41, 639.
Spangled, 1003.
Spell, 154.
Spets, 132.
Sphery, 1021.
Spruce, 985.
Square, 329.
Squint, 413.
Stabled, 534.
Star of Arcady, 341.
State, 35.
Stead, 611.
Step-dame, 830.
Still, 560.
Stoic, 707.
Stops, 345.
Storied, 516.

Straight, 811.
Strook, 301.
Stygian, 132.
Sun-clad, 782.
Sung, 256.
Sure, 148.
Surrounding, 403.
Swain, 497.
Swart, 436.
Swinked, 293.
Sylvan, 268.
Syrups, 674.

T.

Tapestry, 324.
Temple, 461.
Thyrsis, 494.
Timely, 689, 970.
Tinsel-slippered, 877.
To-ruffled, 380.
To seek, 366.
Toy, 502.
Trains, 151.
Treasonous, 702.
Trippings, 961.
Turkis, 894.
Tuscan, 48.
Twain, 284.
Tyrrhene, 49.

U.

Unblenched, 430.
Unenchanted, 395.
Unmuffle, 331.
Unprincipled, 367.
Unweeting, 539.

Unwithdrawing, 711.
Urchin, 845.

V.

Various, 379.
Venturous, 609.
Vermeil-tinctured, 752.
Very, 427.
Vialed, 847.
Viewless, 92.
Violet-embroidered, 233.
Virtue, 165, 621.
Visage, 333.
Vizored, 698.
Votarist, 189.

W.

Wakes, 121.
Warranted, 327.
Wassailers, 179.
Waste, 728, 942.
Weeds, 16.
Welkin, 1015.
What need, 362.
Whilom, 827.
Whit, 774.
Who, 728.
Wily, 151.
Wink, 401.
Wished, 574, 950.
Wizard, 571, 872.
Wont, 332, 549.
Woof, 83.

Y.

Ye, 216.

BIBLIOBAZAAR

The essential book market!

Did you know that you can get any of our titles in large print?

Did you know that we have an ever-growing collection of books in many languages?

**Order online:
www.bibliobazaar.com**

Find all of your favorite classic books!

Stay up to date with the latest government reports!

At BiblioBazaar, we aim to make knowledge more accessible by making thousands of titles available to you-*quickly and affordably*.

Contact us:
BiblioBazaar
PO Box 21206
Charleston, SC 29413

Printed in Great Britain by
Amazon.co.uk, Ltd.,
Marston Gate.